To
Donal and Valerie
Every Good Wish
Bridget O'Hanlon

Widowhood FLYING

Bridget O'Hanlon

Published by Bridget O'Hanlon
Publishing partner: Paragon Publishing, Rothersthorpe
First published 2013

ISBN 978-1-78222-157-9

Book design, layout and production management by Into Print
www.intoprint.net
01604 832149

Printed and bound in UK and USA by Lightning Source

For
my daughter, Joanne Reavell

Contents

About the author

Bridget O'Hanlon is Irish and has lived extensively in England and Australia.

Her stories here entirely fictional and reflect whatever might have caught her interest and attention at any particular time and place.

After a long migration she has happily returned to roost, and is living in Doneraile, North Cork.

Thanksgiving

His fingers fumbled slightly with the catch on the shed door. It was an old looped catch fashioned out of heavy fencing wire, the loop bent with pliers and hammered into the doorjamb and the other loop held to the door with two rusty nails. The closure was simple and effective, he only had to replace the bit of rope on the pin every now and again.

'Gee, Pa,' said Declan, squinting into the gloom, 'you've got enough tools here to open your own shop.' The shed was made of breeze blocks, without a window and the only light came from a missing block on the opposite wall.

'Your grandmother used to have turkeys here,' said Tom. ' She'd fatten them up for Christmas and sell them off. The only way she could make a few bob, those times. I never kept them, nasty, bad tempered things, turkeys. I had a few hens here one time, 'but you could have nothing for the foxes. I got sick of trying to chase the beggars off from the chickens.'

'They were free range then?' said Declan.

'Well, they picked away where they liked in the day, but I put them in here in the night. I closed off that hole when they were in here, but after that I had a sheep, just for keeping the grass down, but your sister wouldn't let me kill it to eat and the bleddy thing died of old age, up there in the acre by the far ditch. Of course, you were gone to America a couple of years that time.' He chuckled at the memory. 'I didn't much bother with livestock after that, only for the old dog, and sure he's as useless as meself.'

'Come on now, Pa,' said Declan, giving his father a friendly punch on the arm, 'don't go selling yourself short. There's plenty of fire left in the belly, now, isn't there?'

'I muddle along anyway,' said Tom. He pushed aside an old

rotary mower. They had come into the shed to find lopping shears. Declan had offered to prune the hedge to save his father from having to climb up on the ladder.

'Climbing the ladder is no problem to him,' his mother had said to him this morning, 'wasn't he up on the roof a month ago, fixing a slate. I told him then he'd kill himself and you know what his answer was? Well, Mary, I can only fall the once. What do you think of that? Eighty-five years of age and no more sense than when he was in short pants. Well, Tom, I said to him, if you're going to fall off the roof, be sure and fall away from the driveway, not to be getting in the way of the ambulance.' She was still laughing when Declan went off to the greenhouse to find his father.

'My God,' Declan cried, turning round in the cramped space, 'I never saw so many tools. You must have dozens of them. They're wonderful, and so old. Forget about the shop, you could open a museum. Do you use all these?'

Tom shifted his cap and scratched his head, looking at the garden tools lined up along the right hand wall of the shed. 'I suppose there's a few of them alright.' He reached forward and picked up a small square spade with a shortish handle. 'This one is a trench spade from the First World War. The soldiers had to carry these to dig the trenches when they got to into position. I bought it in London, just after the Second World War, and brought it back here with me. I still use it; it's great for trenches, exactly what it was made for, but very heavy for such a small spade. You'd be sorry for the lads who had to drag these around with them.'

'You would indeed.' said Declan, stooping to pick up a hoe that had fallen over. 'What's this one for?'

'That now is an onion hoe. It has swan neck for hoeing and cleaning around the onions.'

'I didn't know you had to have a special hoe for onions,' said Declan.

'This one's a Dutch hoe,' said his father, warming to his theme. He was much more comfortable here in the shed examining tools than sitting in the front room with a cup of tea and dainty sandwiches, listening to his son try to explain the dot.com bubble of a couple of years back. 'I was one of the lucky ones,' said Declan, gently patting his crew cut, unconsciously mirroring a gesture of his father's. 'I made my money and got out before the backside fell out of the market.'

'The Dutch hoe, now, has its head angled to rest on the ground while you cut on the push stroke. Very handy for chopping out small roots, or edging, or you can use it as a pry bar. The triangular one here is best when you need to get in deepish. Digs a nice lump out of the soil. See that one there, you won't see too many of those in a garden shed. That's an adze hoe, given to me by a fellow who used to work in the forestry, specially good for deep ground litter; firemen use them too. I have a hand hoe here somewhere,' he said poking around on the floor, 'the hand one has a flared blade sharpened at the bottom and a good way up the sides. I prefer a long handle myself. Look at this one, this is a potato hoe, the handle broke and I made a new one for it out of a lovely piece of ash.' said Tom, and lovingly stroked the smooth handle.

'Enough, already,' said Declan, laughing and raising his hands up in surrender, 'Too much information. That mower must be a hundred years old.'

'It'd be ten, anyway, maybe fifteen. Your man at the pub threw it out and I brought it home and fixed it. Took me three days to get it going, the carburettor kept flooding. But it was worth it, Briggs and Stratton made a very good motor. Ah, there's the pruning shears. I'll just give them a bit of a sharpen and you can lop away to your hearts content.'

They both blinked into the light when they emerged and Declan said, 'speaking of turkeys. I bought a turkey yesterday when I was at the English Market. It's a long time since I saw birds hanging on hooks, with no refrigeration. I guess it won't kill us. I'm going to get Ma to cook it tomorrow for Thanksgiving, and I found a pumpkin too, we'll have all the trimmings.'

As he walked away to fetch the ladder, Tom shook his head at the rasp in his hand and murmured, 'turkey, and it nowhere near Christmas yet,' and shook his head again.

He was busy in the greenhouse that afternoon and refused the afternoon tea in the front room. Declan sat with his mother over her best, and only, bone china tea set. 'Mom, you don't have to go to all this trouble. It'd be much easier for you if we just had a coffee at the kitchen table. You don't have to treat me like a visitor. I'm family.'

'Sure, I don't often get the chance to take out the good ware,' said his mother, flustered. Indeed she was a little nervous of this 'bright shiny son', arriving on their doorstep after so many years. It was as if he reminded her of someone she used to know long ago, and she couldn't find the freckled boy smiling out at her from the faded photographs on the mantelpiece in this sleek, tanned, confident, middle aged man sitting on her old lumpy couch.

'I've just thought of the most amazing present for the old man,' said Declan, reaching for a ham sandwich. ' A ride-on mower!' he announced. 'Isn't that the best idea you ever heard of?'

'A present?' said Mary, 'a ride on mower? But it isn't his birthday for ages.'

'But I won't be here then, Ma, and I want to see his face when I give it to him. I'll make it a thanksgiving present. I'll go out now in the truck and get one immediately.' He bounced off the couch in his enthusiasm, crammed the sandwich in his mouth and headed out the door before his mother could stop him. She sat looking at the tea tray wondering how she was going to get that monstrous turkey into her small gas oven, and worse still, how she was going to tell Tom about the ride-on mower.

'But,' said Tom, 'I don't want a ride on mower. I only have this small bit here to do and I can get the loan of a horse to keep the grass down in the acre now and then.'

'Declan wants to give you something. He wants to make your life easier.' said Mary, wringing her hands. 'Don't say anything to him. Try to look pleased when he brings it back.'

'I don't want it, I tell you.' said Tom, 'I have a grand mower here that will do me the rest of my days. That's a pure waste of money, buying a ride-on mower.'

'He's only doing his best, Tom,' said Mary, 'he says you can get all the mowing done before its time for your coffee in the morning.'

'And what would I be doing with the rest of the day?' asked Tom, once again pushing back his cap to scratch his head. 'I don't understand these new fangled American ways at all.'

'It's a Thanksgiving present,' said Mary desperately.

'Well, I'm not a bit thankful,' roared Tom, and went back into the greenhouse to finish potting his hydrangeas for early flowering.

Some hours later Declan drove back in an empty truck. He slumped into the kitchen and threw himself down on a chair. 'I couldn't get one,' he said, 'I went to four different shops and not one of them would give me the one on the floor, I would have to order one for two weeks time, but I'll be back home by then. I explained and I begged but it was no good, and now I won't have time to organise it before I have to go back home. I certainly wouldn't trust them to order the right one without me keeping an eye on them. I hope you didn't mention it to Pa. I'd hate to raise his hopes and then have to disappoint him.'

He seemed only then to realise that his mother was on her hands and knees in front of the oven with a tape measure in her hand. 'Hell, Ma. What are you doing?' he asked.

'I'm just measuring the oven to make sure that turkey of yours will fit, and I think it's going to be fine. I'll just tie up the legs tight and we should be OK.'

Declan jumped forward to help his mother as she struggled up from the floor.

'Fantastic!' he cried, instantly cheerful again,' we can at least have a proper thanksgiving dinner.'

'That we can, pet,' said Mary, putting her hand to the small of her back and stretching, 'and don't we have plenty to be thankful for?'

Job Security

Nancy shrugged her sequined shoulder and arched an eyebrow at him, gave her hair another glance in the mirror, then teetered off, head held high, to the bar. Mick stared after her for a few seconds, half started towards the main door, hesitated, and then, turning up his collar against the rain, he left the hotel. He hesitated again at the entrance and, as if making a decision, set off towards the bridge. The light canvas shoes he was wearing were not designed for a sudden downpour like this, but Mick hardly noticed. He hunched up his shoulders under a thin jacket and sloshed doggedly through the sudden summer shower. Mr de Silva was going to hear about this.

Just before he reached the bridge he descended sharply into a basement on the left, the steps barely visible beneath a darkened storefront. There was no light or sign to indicate that any business was being conducted there, but when Mick knocked softly on the door, it was immediately opened a couple of inches by a large man in an ill fitting suit, letting a narrow shaft of light brighten the gloom. When he saw Mick, he nodded, opened the door wide and let him in. No words or looks were exchanged between the two men. Mick entered the small dark drinking club and glanced quickly around the bar for his boss. There were a couple of men sitting on stools at either end of the bar nursing drinks and watching a silent game on the television. A working girl was trying to coax a punter in one of the booths to buy a bottle of champagne, but there was no sign of Mr de Silva at his special table facing the door. The jukebox was playing a dreamy dance number but nobody was dancing, and the grimy disco light caught no reflections.

'Just a beer, Eddie', Mick said to the barman, who opened a long neck and placed it on the counter in front of him. 'You seen the boss?' Mick asked. Eddie shook his head. Mick put a note on the damp bar runner, nodded at Eddie and took his drink to a vacant table. He sat under a faded picture of James Dean and Elvis playing pool in a similar barroom to this one. Mick sat looking at the table, cracking his knuckles and ignoring his beer for a few minutes. There was another small rap on the door and Joe, the tall man in the suit, opened the door a crack and then opened it wide to let in a small, rat-faced man in blue jeans and a hooded top, who shook off some of the rain like a wet dog. He noticed Mick and made his way over to the table to slide into the seat opposite. Only then did Mick look up. 'Hello, Lenny', he said, 'you seen the boss?'

'No, Mick, I haven't', said Lenny, 'not since yesterday's job.'

'How'd it go?'

'Won't make me rich anytime soon, that's for sure,' said Lenny, and waited.

'There's none of us getting rich, Lenny. Times are lean.'

When Mick didn't offer him a drink Lenny got up and went to the bar and signalled to Eddie to pour him a small whisky. He searched in a couple of pockets before finding enough coins to pay for the drink. Eddie waited impassively, threw the coins in the drawer and went back to watching the game. Lenny returned to the table and sat down in front of Mick who looked up quickly this time and said in an agitated whisper, 'What about that Nancy, Lenny? You spoken to her lately?'

'No Mick, can't say that I have. Why?'

'She's up to something Lenny. I don't trust her. I'll have to tell the boss to look out for her.'

'What the hell could little Nancy do to Mr de Silva?' asked Lenny. 'She's just a singer in a bar.'

'She says she's got connections,' said Mick, looking around to make sure nobody could hear him. 'She said there's a big job coming up and did I want in'

As he spoke the tall doorman came over and motioned to the other seat at the table. Mick nodded, and the doorman sat down.

'Quiet night, Joe,' said Lenny.

'You know Mondays,' said Joe, and then, looking at Mick, 'What's up?'

Mick looked around the bar again. 'I'm looking for Mr de Silva. I have information that he would find valuable.'

'What kind of valuable?' asked Joe.

'That Nancy', said Mick.

'The singer?' asked Joe.

'Yeah, the singer. She says the boss is finished.'

'When did she say that?' asked Joe.

'Just now. I saw her at the Del Rio. She was between sets. She said that de Silva is all washed up and that her and Bobby are taking over the territory. She offered me in on a job coming up soon.'

'No kidding,' said Joe. 'She'd want to watch that pretty little neck of hers. The boss can eat bits of girls like her before breakfast, and that Bobby, he's just a blow in.'

'And a blow hard, by the sound of him,' said Lenny. 'I've never even seen him. What did he ever do? Mr de Silva's run this turf for twenty years.'

'Well, Nancy says it's time for a change of guard, and I can be in, or I can be out. It's up to me,' said Mick. 'I need to warn Mr de Silva. I don't trust her or that Bobby.'

'Yeah, we'd better,' said Lenny. 'Mr de Silva always rewards loyalty.' He looked hopefully at Joe who made no move to go to the bar even when Lenny rolled his empty glass around on the table. He sighed and leaned back in his chair. 'The boss will soon put them in their place.'

Mick took a small sip from his bottle as Joe responded to another rap on the door. This time the door was pushed open by a wild haired young man who rushed in, dripping rain all over the wooden floor. 'Mick here?' he asked Joe. Joe turned and pointed and then followed the younger man as he hurried over.

'Mick,' he cried. 'Did you hear?' All eyes at the bar turned towards him.

'Hear what?' said Mick mirroring the alarm on the young man's face.

'Mr de Silva,' Paulie cried, 'they just dragged his body out of the river, not half an hour ago. Stone dead.'

All heads turned towards him as Paulie spoke and the only sound was from the jukebox as it slid the finished record back into the stack.

Mick glared around the bar and the other patrons dropped their gaze and went back to what they were doing. Nobody spoke for a few seconds and then Mick and Lenny burst on Paulie with questions. 'Dead? What happened? Did he fall in? No! Are they sure? Who did it? What do the police say? No witnesses?

'Who told you?' asked Mick.

'I heard it on the square not five minutes ago. Big crowd near the bridge. The cops are swarming, blue lights everywhere, and two ambulances. Too late for the ambulance, though. I got the hell out of there before I was spotted.'

Gradually the men around the table went quiet. Joe said, 'I think we need a drink.' He caught the barman's eye. Eddie brought a bottle of Scotch and glasses to the table, set them down and stepped back looking from one to another. When nobody spoke he went back behind the bar.

As Lenny reached for the bottle to pour the drinks he asked, 'What are we going to do?'

'You don't think Bobby did it, do you?' Mick asked Joe. 'Do you think Nancy knew he was gone when she spoke to me tonight?'

Joe shrugged, and the four men silently contemplated their drinks. 'He was a fine man,' said Lenny at last. 'We're going to miss him,' added Paulie.

'We're out of a job, you mean,' said Mick, bitterly, suddenly loud. 'What are we going to do now?'

Joe went over to the bar and turned the television off. A mark of respect. Nobody objected. He went back to the table and the three men looked up at him. He shrugged again. 'Maybe you need to think about her offer, Mick,' he said.

'Don't do it!' cried Paulie.

'I gotta live,' said Mick sourly.

'Well, if you're going, I'm going too,' said Lenny, filling up his glass again. 'What about you, Joe?'

'I'll see,' said Joe. 'I'll have to see what happens to the club,' He waved his hand vaguely round the shabby little bar. 'I'll be needed here till things are, you know, sorted out.'

'You'd better stick with us, Paulie,' said Mick, 'unless you've got a better idea.'

Paulie shook his heady slowly. 'I don't know Mick. I think I'd better keep my head down for a while. I might stay here with Joe.' He looked up at the tall man beside him, who inclined his head a fraction.

After another long pause Mick sat up, pushed his drink away and squared his shoulders. 'OK, boys, let's get it over with', he said. 'Let's go and see her and see if she can put in a good word for us with Bobby. Farewell Mr de Silva,' and he gave a mock salute towards his boss's usual table.

Lenny finished his drink and eyed Mick's discarded whisky, but reluctantly left it where it was. The two scraped back their chairs and shuffled out the door without another word.

Joe closed and bolted the door after them and reached inside his jacket for his phone. He flipped the phone open, dialled a number and said softly, 'They're on their way, Boss. Yeah. Swallowed it whole.' Then he flipped the phone shut and gave young Paulie a slap on the shoulder. He signalled to the barman to turn the game back on and walked casually over to the jukebox.

'Hey, Eddie,' he called over his shoulder to the barman, 'got any coins for this thing?'

Day Three

By nightfall on the third day, Wayne had melted into his fear. Trying to calm the children had taken more energy than he had to spare. They were all, along with the dog, sheltering under the Land Rover, the only shade in sight.

They had broken down on the way back to the homestead, from a neighbouring settlement to recruit stockmen to move the herd. They were half a day from home when the vehicle bogged in a dry creek bed. Attempts to move it had only lodged it deeper into the powdery earth.

He stood motionless to scan the horizon. Flies crawled across his face, and drank from the corner of his eyes. Across the treeless plain he searched for dust plumes from a vehicle. All he could see, through the shimmer of sun on limestone, was saltbush and low myall acacias. Yesterday he made a cross out of white stones, in case of an aerial search, finishing by first light, before the heat sapped his failing strength. A day and a half trip, and he had failed to take enough provisions. Water had been rationed from the first day, and what little food they had was gone by the middle of the second. The children, parched and exhausted, were quiet now; the dog hardly moved and his panting was shallow.

Wayne had a torch ready for signalling, he had built a fire to create smoke, and kept a mirror in his pocket to catch the light and attract attention, but there was no one to signal, the skies were insistently blue and empty, and the desert dust swirled in the breeze.

The dog suddenly stirred, looking towards the west. The children rose, and stood with their father watching as the dog raced off, barking hoarsely, into the scrub.

Bingo

MONDAY MORNING and dry after the night rain. No doubt the rain would start again soon; the ground was drenched; the rain barrels overflowing. Where the concrete on the back path was uneven and cracked, broken here and there from years of use, small puddles formed. If we ever see the sun again, he thought, I must do something about that path. He turned his face to the wall and pulled the blanket closer around his shoulders. He stared blankly at the faded wallpaper near his face. As a boy, sick in bed, he used to count the roses on each strip of wallpaper, then the leaves and then the stalks. He did this over and over, fretting if the numbers weren't the same, because then he would have to start all over again to make the counting right. Later, his reading told him that this counting was like a transcendental mantra, focussing the mind to bar the way of stray thoughts. As far as he could see, the counting was just a way of not thinking at all, and had become such a habit now, he started every day with an inventory of the window panes and angles and frames of the room, having graduated from roses through many a bitter winter. He was more interested now in the conformity of the stripes on the curtains, beige and salmon pink, alternating with clusters of green diamond shapes. They could do with a wash, too, he thought sourly, and turned again to face the room.

Through the thin wall, he could hear his mother stirring in her sleep. As soon as he could tell she was reaching wakefulness, he would go downstairs and lay out her breakfast and her tablets. She had medication to take each morning, and if it was on the table when she came into the kitchen she might overlook the fact that he had put them out. If she saw him struggling with the blister packs with his thick fingers she became greatly agitated. 'I suppose you *have* to fiddle and fumble about like a big oaf when you know I am perfectly well able to get my own tablets out. Haven't I been doing it for years? I'm not a complete fool, you know.'

He had long passed the point of commenting or even answering when her tone was such. The doctor had made him promise that he would make sure his mother had the right medicines at the right time, and he performed this duty with stubborn dedication, in the face of her disapproval. It was much easier to get down before her and lay them out, he had discovered, and have the table set and the kettle on. That seemed to put her in a reasonable frame of mind, and an incident could be averted. Averting incidents had become his life's work since his father had died four years before. The old man would roar at her when she started her 'nonsense', as they secretly called it between them, and she would quieten quickly enough, content to sniff, and to mumble her woes into the kitchen sink.

When he could hear her rousing herself , he pulled on his old dressing gown and shuffled down the stairs to light the fire in the kitchen. This was where his mother preferred to spend most of her day, going through old photographs and sighing over the good old days, before the Lord took her husband from her, or listening to the local radio to see who had died in the night. Sometimes she liked to read the paper or a magazine. When he saw her getting down the scissors to cut out the specials at the supermarket from the paper, he knew he had some time to himself and took off to the barn where he was restoring a 1963 MG, the love of his life. Might as well be anyway, he said to himself, fat chance of meeting a woman, when he hardly ever got outside the house except for Mass and the groceries.

'Are you still thinking of going to the Bingo on Friday, Ma?' he asked as she came into the kitchen.

'Would I be able to get a sup of tea into my mouth, do you think, before you try to race me out the door to waste money I don't have on gambling that the good Lord frowns deeply on.'

'I doubt, now Ma, if God would think Bingo was a mortal sin, especially when it's held in the church hall.'

'Much you'd know about what God would think.' she huffed, 'Is that egg boiled yet?' They sat at the table in silence and ate their eggs and bread and butter and shop bought marmalade, washed down with strong, scalding tea, the way they both liked it. He silently counted the cups hanging on the dresser and the plates standing on the top shelf. He had just started on the pens in the bowl on the windowsill when there was a rap at the door.

Their neighbour, Nell, had been trying to get his mother to go to the Bingo for some time, and he sensed a weakening in the force of her refusals. An outing would be good for her; she was too much cut off from the outside world since his father died.

'Here's Nell now,' he cried with forced enthusiasm, and rushed to open the door.

'Come in Nell, God love you, you must be soaked,' his mother cried, equally jolly. 'Get Nell a cup of tea there, Tom. Sit down here Nell. Did you bring more magazines? You're very good.' He pulled up another chair and poured the tea as the two women began to exchange news.

'Archie Brown is very sick with the gout. He was taken in to the hospital yesterday. The pain is something fierce. Mary said he'll be there for a week at least. said Nell. 'But Noel Buckley is home now from his daughter's in England, and as well as ever he was before Eileen passed away. He's been gone nearly a year, would you ever think it? I don't know what happens to the time.'

Tom let his mind drift away as the women chatted, and then roused himself to bring in sticks for the sitting room fire. If his mother would ever go to the bingo then he could go to the dance at the hotel. Friday was a good night, his cousin told him, and he was desperate to talk about something other than the old days or the shocking price of everything. Not to mention being surrounded by beautiful women, one of whom might one day look kindly on him. God knows, he thought, it's that long since I spoke to a woman my own age I wouldn't have a clue what to say to her. I doubt she'd have much interest in the carburettor I'm having trouble with just now. Suppose, he thought, I've lost the power of speech, I go up to a girl to ask for a dance an open my mouth and no words come out? He was about to break out in an anxious sweat when he heard the magic word.

'Bingo?' said his mother, as if the word was entirely new to her.

'Yes,' said Nell, leaning forward to her friend, 'Friday night in the hall. Only a fiver for the whole night and tea and biscuits in the interval. Good prizes too, and Eamon is a scream when he's calling the numbers. Clickety click; two fat ladies.' She leaned back in her chair and laughed.

'What kind of talk is that,' his mother cried, ' two fat ladies?'

'Oh, don't mind it Betty, it's only bingo talk for eighty eight, like two fat ladies, get it? And Clickety click is sixty six. He calls out the number too, so you wouldn't have to worry about not knowing the slang. The evening just flies.' She still had the smile on her face and he could see his mother's indignation subside a little. 'And now that Noel Buckley's back, he can take us in his car,' Nell rushed on, sensing her advantage, 'Wouldn't it be lovely?' and with a wink to Tom, ' I'd even let you sit in the front with Noel.'

'Indeed, I would not be sitting in the front of a car with a man I hardly know.' said Betty, grasping at another obstacle to the outing.

'Get away with you,' said Nell, laughing again, 'you've known Noel Buckley for as long as you've known me, all your life, in fact.' She took a sip of her tea, and Tom waited. When she put the cup down, she said, 'you'll come then, Friday night? Oh, go on Betty, it'll do you good, and I'd love the company.'

'Well, I'll think about it.' Said Betty, giving her shoulders a little shake. Tom let his breath go and left the room and went about his chores. That was as much of an answer that Nell would get for the moment, and it was progress of sorts. As he started to sweep the porch his reverie returned, and he did a little waltz around with the yard broom. He had gradually assumed most of the jobs around the house, as his mother could not bear the thought of any strange woman from the home help coming in, poking though her things, and telling the whole place what she had. I wonder, he thought, if that quiet, dark haired girl from the post office goes to the dance.

Wednesday was mostly spent in the garden. Tom kept a fine vegetable garden and Betty spent the morning tending the flowers and waging a constant, losing battle with the dandelions. She had lost patience with her knitting and other things she used to enjoy. Then it was time for Tom to get the dinner, after which she had a snooze in the chair beside the fire while Tom resumed his own battle with the carburettor. Thursday was their shopping day, where the battleground moved to the checkout, and then they went into the hotel for a 'decent meal for a change' as she always said.

On Friday morning he woke with the light, as usual. He'd been reading an article in a magazine, all about photography and how the light was better in the morning and evening for taking pictures of plants and flowers, and birds if you could get close enough, and keep still enough. He thought he'd have the patience for that, and kept meaning to get out his father's old camera and have a go, but when he opened his eyes to the morning he never remembered the flowers and birds, just the number of stripes on the curtains and his mother stirring in the next room.

This particular morning was cooler than he'd expected and he decided to build up the fire well in the kitchen before his mother came down. He was busy with this as she came into the room. She took a deep breath and addressed Tom's back, saying, 'I was thinking, I might give the bingo a try tonight, just to please Nell, you know.'

'Thanks be to God,' said Tom in a rush.

She whirled around, faster than he could have thought possible. '*What* did you say?' she demanded.

'Thanks be to God, Mother, I managed to get this blasted fire going. The wood's so wet, I was afraid it wouldn't take.' He noisily aimed coal expertly to the back of the grate, 'Bingo, you say, well now that might be nice. Nell will be pleased,' he said and headed off out the back door with the empty coal bucket.

Winter Caller

It was early in the New Year that I saw a solitary figure approach the house, buffeted mercilessly by the worst weather we had seen so far that winter. He was pushing hard against the snow and swirling wind, with great power and determination. I recall wondering who could possibly be abroad, and on foot, in such inclemency. I could just discern him from the library window. I assumed it to be a man, although all I could see at first was a dark shape moving slowly along the driveway to the house, leaning forward, thrusting his way through the maelstrom that tried to drive him back. It would hardly be a woman out there in the snow, unaccompanied and unattended, in such weather. I took little mind of the traveller. It was not unknown for peddlers and such to travel the countryside, and he would surely soon veer off toward the stables for warmth and to beg some food from the cook.

My leisure was in studying, in what little time I had to spare from the affairs of my estate, the work of Euripides, being very fond of the Greek dramatists. I was currently reading 'The Trojan Women', a play he had written in the aftermath of the Athenians attack on the island of Melos, and expressing his revulsion at their actions and the inclusion of women and children as casualties of war. I was also closely following the sporadic news brought from the capital on the war now raging in Europe.

I was warming myself at the fire, and working my way through the second act of the play when Bates knocked on the library door.

'There's a gentleman outside, sir, asking for you,' he said as he advanced into the room. 'I was inclined at first to send him around the back to the kitchen, but he asked for you by name.'

'Who is it Bates?' I demanded, not well pleased to be interrupted from my reading.

' He says his name is Smith, sir, Victor Smith, and that he is not known to you but has travelled a long way to meet with you. He knew your name, sir.' Bates repeated.

'What class of a fellow is he then?' I asked.

'Oh, a gentleman, sir, clearly, very mannerly and very well spoken,' said Bates.

'Oh, very well,' I said, 'Show him in.'

Bates withdrew and returned a moment later, sooner than I had expected, followed noiselessly by a tall man with a dark cloak gathered around him. I was a little taken aback to note that his head was still covered and I could not see his face. He must have divined my expression because he immediately threw off the cloak from his head sending flakes of snow scattering across the rug.

'Excuse me, Mr Lambert,' he cried, stepping past Bates before he could be announced, and holding out his hand to me, 'Excuse me, dear sir, for interrupting your morning meditations.' I was looking into an open, friendly face, which was smiling as much as his frozen features would allow. I extended my hand a little hesitantly and he grasped it in both of his, squeezing it vigorously between his freezing fingers. The iciness of his grip sent a jolt through me, and made me shiver involuntarily. He immediately let go of my hand and said, 'I beg your pardon, sir. I seem to have left my gloves at the great house during my visit to your neighbour, Lord Danbury. I hope I do not shock you, with my sudden appearance and my deathly cold grip.'

I recovered my wits as I looked into his candid, pleasant face. 'Not at all, um, Mr Smith,' I said, 'come and stand nearer to the fire. How is Lord Danbury? I haven't seen him since he was brought down with the gout. Bates, get Mr Smith a draught to ease his cold.'

Mr Smith strode gladly to stand before the blaze and chafed some life back into his hands. 'Lord Danbury is not so well, I have to tell you. I suspect his time is not far off,' he threw at me over his shoulder, and I mumbled my regrets.

Then he turned, and with his back to the fire, surveyed the library with great interest. He seemed perfectly at ease, and in no way hurrying to explain the purpose of his visit or how he came to know of me.

'But sir,' he cried, spying my book, open on the table beside a chair, 'I am interrupting you from your work. I do apologise once more.'

'Not at all, Mr Smith,' I replied. Now that the visitor had made himself more comfortable, my mild resentment at the intrusion was giving way to curiosity and the prospect of conversation. We had very few visitors during the winter, and my poor wife worried that I lacked society as she was kept to her bed most days. This stranger may have news from the front; he may even be able to bring word of the Emperor's downfall. God knows, I thought, this terrible war must end soon. I had long since given over cursing the wounded leg that prevented me from joining the conflict. 'I was merely revisiting a play from Euripides of which I am particularly fond.'

Mr Smith glanced down at the open book, 'Ah yes, our friend Euripides, a gloomy chap, don't you think?' and he leaned back, put one hand inside his jacket in a parody of Napoleon and quoted from an earlier work of the playwright's, 'And now you know; Life is held on loan. The price of life is death,' He intoned this in his deep, warm voice, waving his free hand outward toward the imaginary amphitheatre. He looked over at me laughing, and I could not but join him in his mirth. What a splendid fellow. This day was turning out to be much better that its portend. A pleasant visitor, and a classicist to boot.

Bates entered after a soft knock, with a tray of glasses and a pitcher of mulled wine to ward off the cold. 'Ah,' cried my erudite guest, 'a warming cup of Hipocris,' making reference to an alternate name given the drink in honour of Hippocrates' and its reputed health giving properties. Bates had also brought some cold meats and bread for Mr Smith, assuming him to be hungry. At another time I may have been angry at Bates' offering sustenance without my direction, but in this instance I was warming to my guest and anxious to make him as much at ease as possible, so that we might have some conversation. I had completely forgotten to seek the purpose of his visit. He thanked the butler rather more profusely than was necessary, and Bates backed away from the table, beaming.

After Mr Smith had sipped some wine, and refused all victuals, I ventured to enquire of his provenance. He was from an estate down the country, he told me, and had travelled north to see Lord Danbury, who had mentioned my name, as a noted classical scholar. I demurred at this flattering title, but we soon were in the deepest and most earnest of conversations concerning matters of interest to us both. When Bates came to advise us that luncheon was served I was amazed to find that the morning had sped by so swiftly. Mr Smith continued to refuse food, and I, being much taken with my visitor, declined also to leave the warmth and conviviality of the library. Bates informed me that my wife, having felt unable to come down for the meal, was being served hot broth in her chambers, and our daughter, Isobel, would eat with her governess in the nursery.

After we had some discussion on the master tragedians of the ancient world, our discourse turned quite naturally to the war, and here Mr Smith turned out to be a harbinger of extensive intelligence.

The might of the British navy, he told me, had been sorely challenged by Napoleon, who had amassed a huge army at Boulogne in preparation for an invasion of England. But his attempts to cut Britain off from Europe, thereby curtailing her powerful trade there, had failed and the Royal Navy had put an abrupt end to Napoleon's ambitions. The Emperor had recently crushed the Prussians at the battle of Jena, so there was no clear prospect of victory for either side.

As grave as this news was, it was some comfort to know that England seemed to be wearing down the military might of France somewhat. I asked how much of the fighting Mr Smith had seen.

'Oh, my dear fellow,' he sighed, 'I have spent the entire conflict travelling to tend the sick and wounded in such far flung places as Egypt and Russia.' He waved an arm towards the window and laughing, said, 'such weather as yours is no shock to one who has endured a Russian winter.'

'You must be a medic then,' I said,' or a chaplain.'

'No, my good sir, no such vital, healing role for me, I'm afraid. I just do what I can for those who need comfort.' At this he quietened, and we both sat looking into the embers of the fire, pondering the ravages of battle.

I was on the point of insisting that he change into some spare clothes of mine and let the housekeeper dry his own, when Isobel burst through the door and ran across the room, bringing the chill of the outdoors with her, just as Mr Smith had done earlier. Her face was flushed with excitement, and the hood to her cloak and her fur gloves were covered in snow.

'Whoa, there,' I cried, smiling down at her, delighting in her pleasure.

'Oh,' cried her governess, rushing in behind Isobel, 'I do apologise Mr Lambert, sir. She got away from me, she was so excited.'

'No, Miss Freeth, no, let me. Let me tell him. Daddy, you must come and see my snowman. I made him myself with a carrot for a nose and cinders for a mouth and eyes. You must come at once before he melts.'

'Not much danger of him melting in this weather,' I said, laughing. She led a very quiet life, my darling child, with no brothers or sisters to play with, and her mother sickly more often than not. I was most often occupied and her governess was a dour woman who rarely smiled.

My guest had moved away when Isobel came in, but now, as he came forward from the shadows, Isobel gave a start when she realised I was not alone, and rushed to me, hiding her face in my jacket.

'It's all right, poppet,' I said, ruffling her hair. 'Mr Smith is something of a snowman too. And I'm not at all sure that you should be outside in this.' I was concerned for her health, but reluctant to spoil her game. The governess made to apologise again, but I waved her away.

Mr Smith advanced quietly towards us and Isobel looked up at him bashfully through her lashes. When he had approached her, he crouched down until he was at eye level to her, looking at her flushed face. She looked straight at him now, smiling, all shyness gone.

'Yes, my poor child,' he said gently, 'you'll catch your death.'

Oh, the Tomato

Scent of musk pervades the air;
Gleams of sunlight here and there
Sifted through the wavery glass;
Peeping orbs appear at last.

Measure plant food carefully,
Fill the bucket reverently,
Gently douse the tender roots.
Summer heralds plump, red fruits.

Vine or Beefsteak, sweet Cherrola;
Balconi; Venus, Tigerella,
Falconorossa, Tumbling Tom;
Moneymaker – bring 'em on.

Pomodora, Orange Pixie;
Strawberry Tiger, Sleeping Lady.
Living Legend, Sweet Losetto,
How we love our dear tomato.

Widowhood Flying

'Just as well I haven't got a smoke, anyway,' he mumbled.

'Why's that then?' asked Jim.

'Wouldn't be able to light the bastard in this rain,' said Ronnie and they both snorted a laugh, muffled by the downpour battering their ramshackle dug out. The jungle around them reverberated with night noises; all the nocturnal scratchings and hoots just a dimly heard undercurrent to the rain slapping the palms.

'Could do with one anyway. These leeches are bleeding me dry. They're down my boots now.' said Jim.

'Nah, that's for ticks, not leeches. You can burn a tick off with the end of your smoke. Leeches need to be eased off with a knife or they'll just keep on sucking till they plop off, full as a drum.'

'Supposed to stop raining by the end of March,' said Jim.

'We should be so lucky,' said Ronnie, refusing to be cheered. They did not speak much after that, each lost in his own wretched reverie.

Later they watched as a small bunch of new recruits stumbled through the trees, dragged sideways by the weight of their knapsacks, 'Look at that,' their sergeant roared pointing at one of the advancing men, 'That boy there looks about twelve, for Chrissake,' He spat on the ground in disgust. 'How the hell did you get through, then? What school did they kidnap you from, eh sonny? They'll be dragging kids out of their prams next and sending them up here with their nappies hanging off their arses,' Sam Turner came to a halt in front of him, a half smile on his face, not sure if the sergeant was joking. The sergeant spat again and grunted to them to go and stow their gear anywhere dry they could find.

'And where might that be, sarge?' asked Ronnie when the lads were out of earshot.

'Go and check on the pigeons, Thompson, and give your mouth a rest,' said the sergeant, and Ronnie limped through the sludge to the communications tent. Since his injury he had spent most of his time with the lofts, feeding and cleaning up after the birds. The pigeon handler assigned to their troop had been killed early in the action and Ronnie had learned enough to take over the job. They relied on the pigeons to carry messages, and sometimes photographs, to and from Port Moresby or Bootless Bay. The typhoons, the rain and treacherous mountain ranges in this part of Papua New Guinea made normal wireless transmissions unreliable if not totally useless.

'It's not for the love of nature that I spend so much time in here,' Ronnie told Sam when he looked in one day to see what was going on. 'These birds often mean the difference between life and death to us squaddies stuck here on the track. Bloody little miracles they are. A hand full of feed and a scratch behind the ear and this little blighter will get a message back to base quicker than you could drive it, if you had anything to drive that is; if there were any bloody roads to drive on. Sixty miles an hour they go. Can you believe that? My old man's got a Chrysler that would fall to bits if you expected it to do that; if he had any petrol to put in it, that is. The brass thought they'd gone back to the middle ages when the pigeons were brought in, but they've saved more lives that you could count.' He busied himself changing water and filling feed troughs and cleaning out the rattan cages, all the while soothing the sharp-eyed birds who murmured back to him. Sam followed him around for a while helping.

'Bet you didn't think you'd come all the way up the Kokoda trail to wipe up pigeon shit, did you, lad?' said Ronnie.

Sam turned to him, excited, 'Have you seen much action, Ronnie?'

'A damn sight more than I'd like. And you needn't look at me like that, either. We spend most of the time soaked to the skin and half starved, and every now and then, when the enemy's on the move we're scared out of our wits. No glory here, old son, just boredom and misery sprinkled with big doses of shit-scared every now and again.' When he saw the light drain out if the boy's eyes he went on, 'don't mind me, Sam, I've been stuck up here too long. You'll see plenty of action soon enough. Any day now we'll get word of Japanese troop movements and then we'll be armed and at 'em.'

Sam searched for a safer topic to soften the conversation, and pointed at the pigeons. 'Why don't they just take off and fly anywhere they like, then?'

'They're proper trained homing pigeons,' said Ronnie, also glad of the change of subject, 'some of them do get lost, of course, but not many. The hens are more steady, more reliable if you like,' he risked a sly grin, ' the cock birds need a bit more incentive. With the fellas, what some handlers do is leave them in with the hen for a few minutes before they are transported and then when they're let off, they are doubly keen to get home, back to the hen. It's called widowhood flying.' He turned, smiling, 'Bit like us, aren't they? Anxious to get home to the missus. You got a girl, Sam? Waiting for you in Melbourne?'

Sam blushed and shuffled his feet. 'No one special,' he said.

'Never you mind, lad. Wait till you're strolling down Lygon Street in your dress uniform, with your medals shining brighter than the girls' eyes. You'll have to beat them of with a stick,' he said and they both laughed.

Jim had sidled in behind them. 'There's supplies just got here,' he said, and they went outside to see the arrival of the native carriers, laden with food, blankets and other equipment, which they dumped in front of the supply tent before collapsing on the ground. The camp cook hurried over to the carriers with water canteens and their meagre ration of rice. A few other men locked ravaged eyes on the bundles, praying for mail and food, willing the sergeant to hurry as he marked off the ammunition.

'These are our other saviours,' Ronnie said, indicating the men prone on the ground, too tired to gasp for breath. 'A bloke wrote a poem about them a couple of years ago, famous it is. When we came first we stole all their crops and flattened their villages.'

'Why do they help us then?' said Sam.

'Because the Japs were worse, mate, the Japs were worse.' He pointed to the carriers' frizzy, matted hair, overhanging their tattooed faces, 'Fuzzy Wuzzie Angels, we call them. Without them and the pigeons we'd have been tucker for the crows months ago.'

The rain stopped at the end of March as expected, stopped like a fire hydrant being turned off, and now the sun lashed them, lifting the rain from the forest to create a mosquito-ridden miasma that made them more sore and exhausted. Troop movements increased, the Japanese were slashing their way further down the track, through the Owen Stanley Ranges, towards Port Moresby. Day and night they could hear shelling and gunfire, echoing off the walls of the jungle. Battle was imminent, and the men were restless, waiting for the order to march; the stench of dirt and decay in the camp mingled with the smell of excitement and fear.

Ronnie gnawed at his knuckles in frustration and also in smothered relief. Only he and the cook had been left in camp, unfit for battle. Ronnie shambled around the lofts explaining to the pigeons, in great detail, the horrors of the mountain track the soldiers had to fight their way through to even get close to the enemy; the altitude on the ridges; the tangled trees and vines; the torment of the insects, and the dumps of putrefying food and dead bodies lining the trail, a track totally impassable by motor vehicles, hacked by the locals just wide enough for the sick and wounded to stumble along.

Down these tracks the native carriers took injured soldiers to Ower's Corner, for help or burial. They rejected the army issue stretchers as useless for the conditions, too straight, too rigid, liable to toss a sick man into the scrub. Instead they improvised their own, one or two blankets bound with string and vines to two long poles carried by as many as eight bearers, travelling over ground that the Aussies considered impassable, and moving as smoothly and gently as silk sheets caressing bare skin.

And down these tracks the native carriers took Sam Turner, blood oozing steadily from the wound in his abdomen, sweat beading on his twisted features, and confusion clouding his eyes.

'Hold on, son,' Jim had told him, 'they'll have you back up here in this cesspit in no time.'

The sergeant read out the message that young private Sam Turner hadn't reached base alive; that the usual telegram would be sent to his parents. Ronnie started cursing, low and slow and hard, every foul word he could think, of repeated until he ran out of breath and then he started again. Jim stood like a statue staring at nothing, his bottom teeth nibbling at his moustache, face blotchy and glistening.

More time passed, more men were wounded, more died; some fell from the bush typhoid that even the local inhabitants had no defence against. The explosion of shells punctuated the drone of aircraft. Worn and haggard, the dwindling squad staggered from one skirmish to the next, holding their position to the death, and sleeping when and where they dropped.

Just before dawn, after the latest battering night, Jim shook him roughly from a fitful doze. 'Hey, Ron, wake up. There's a pigeon just come from Bootless Bay. The sarge wants us lined up, quick smart. Maybe the war's over.' he grinned through stained teeth.

'Yes, mate,' said Ronnie, stiffly raising his head, 'and mybe my old man's the Archbishop.'

'Righto you lot. Stand to attention,' roared the sergeant, and the men shuffled their feet. 'I got good news and I got bad news,' he leered at them. 'The bad news is,' and he paused, scanning the few remnants of the squad before him 'the bad news is that you're the dirtiest, scruffiest looking bunch I've ever had the misfortune to lead,' his voice rasping through the undergrowth. A couple of the younger lads at the back attempted to straighten up.

'And the good news, you miserable shower,' he paused again, but the grin was spreading across his face, and he waved the message over his head, 'we're going home! It's over. The Japs are done for,' and he threw the scrap of paper up in the air and held his arms high in a victorious salute. The men stared at him in silence for seconds, and then the roars and whoops, and a bit of singing started. Men hugged each other and cried, they hugged the sergeant, they hugged the carriers. They would have hugged the pigeons if Ronnie had not guarded the lofts.

The packing up was quicker now, the dust and flies ignored, debris tossed aside and letters from home tucked into uniform pockets. The last pigeon was standing by to send word of their readiness to move out.

Ronnie brought the cage out. Some of the men took off their caps and clutched them to their chests. He whispered to the pigeon, 'This is for Sam and all the other lads,' and then, with a flourish, opened the cage to release her. They shaded their eyes to follow her flight. She whirled and faltered and then, gaining confidence, headed south, getting higher and smaller in the violet sky. And they craned their necks and watched and watched until their eyes watered.

Clearing the Slate

Ambrose owned one of the first motorcars to be seen in the village, although he did not quite own it yet. By a protracted means of threats, promises and pleading he had managed to amass sufficient money to pay Jimmy Hogan, Produce Merchant, a down payment on the old Ford which was to lift his fortunes. He had, wisely, he explained to Clancy over a comforting pint, ' anticipated the growing demand for the pleasures of the internal combustion engine and now only fame and prosperity could follow.'

When he got home later, he explained his plan to his wife while she kneaded dough.

'I can make a fine living, Margaret, taking people wherever they want to go, in fabulous comfort and stupendous speed.' He linked his thumbs in his braces and gazed fondly at the car sitting outside the front door. 'The horse and trap is dead, Margaret. Speed and convenience are the order of the day. The motor car will release us from the indignity and drudgery of our former lives.'

'You have enough taken tonight, Ambrose,' said Margaret.

'You mark my words, my girl. I'll have a fleet of them on the road before you can blink, and we'll be off the slate in no time.'

'We'll see,' said Margaret, well aware of the length of the slate and the length of no time.

'Only today Sister Mary Agnes was making tentative enquiries about tariffs.'

'Tariffs, how are you,' said Margaret. 'What would the nuns be wanting with a motor car?'

'A jaunt,' he cried, 'An American tourist. Bulging with money, the Yanks. Wanting to see the auld country.'

'Another nun, is it?'

'Indeed it is, and looking to hire a fine, reliable man to take her around and find her roots and, now how did she say it? Ah yes, 'imbibe the flavour of original Ireland.''

'She'd be better off imbibing the flavour of original sin,' said Clancy, who had somehow managed to steal in and sit himself closer to the fire than anybody else.

'She can imbibe whatever she likes,' said Ambrose, 'American money is as good as any, and there's a lot more of it, I think. I have arranged an appropriate voyage of discovery which is to commence at nine o'clock this coming Tuesday morning.' On which note he remembered their straitened circumstances and sank his teeth into the soda bread Margaret had made for supper. Imminent wealth notwithstanding, meat might be a while away yet.

Tuesday arrived cool and drizzling. The Ford gleamed in Ambrose's eye. 'The finest vehicle in all Ireland,' he cried, resplendent in his best and only suit, 'sweet Mary and Joseph will bless this day.'

'Have you enough petrol?' asked Margaret.

'Good grief, woman, aren't I embarking on an illustrious career? Would I overlook the merest detail?' cried Ambrose as he polished the gleaming bonnet with the underside of his left sleeve.

'You should take some food.'

'That will not be necessary. The messengers of the Lord will not overlook the sustenance of the beleaguered.'

'Ah, but will they give you any?' asked Clancy, warming his hands at the fire.

'Get away from me, Clancy. I'm a busy man,' said Ambrose as he strode from the house, settled himself carefully behind the wheel, drew on his yellow calfskin gloves and, with a grand wave to the neighbours, drove away.

The two nuns emerged smiling from the convent porch where they had been waiting for the car.

'Mr O'Rourke, I am delighted to meet you. I have been so looking forward to this day,' said Sister Theresa from Boston.

'I am at your disposal, sister,' beamed Ambrose, his chest swollen with pride and moment.

'Well now, Ambrose dear,' said Sister Mary Agnes, who had known him since he was a small boy, 'we'll pop into the church at Mallow and take Sister over to Mourne Abbey and perhaps, if we have the time, a small visit to Blarney Castle, not to kiss the stone, you understand, and then back to Killavullen where Sister's grandmother went to school, and a glimpse of the Blackwater River down near Bridgetown Abbey would be grand.' She hardly paused for breath as Ambrose led them gently towards the waiting car.

'Your carriage awaits, ladies,' he swept an imaginary hat from his head in a low bow, ' and you mustn't worry about a thing. It's a grand day and the good Lord will bless our travels.' He closed the door for Sister Teresa and rushed round the car to usher Sister Mary Agnes to her seat, breathing in deeply, as he did so, the rich warm smell of polished leather. Giving a last, swift, surreptitious rub with his sleeve to a nearby sliver of chrome, he settled himself into the driver's seat and pointed the Ford in the direction of his prospects.

'God bless you, Mr O'Rourke,' murmured Sister Theresa.

It was indeed a grand day. The rain had stopped, the sun squeezed a look at them every now and again and the car never faltered. Ambrose was in his heaven. A wonderful start to his new career. The priest would hear of this. Monsignors would press for his services. Trips to Cork and Dublin would follow. Prelates would recline in the musky comfort of his wonderful vehicle and marvel at this confident command of the wheel. There would be masses said for Ambrose O'Rourke and Henry Ford, great men. Debt would be behind him. He would be able to buy a proper uniform and clear the slate.

After midday they stopped for lunch, a pleasant, light meal, provided by the convent, which the nuns shared with Ambrose, as he had been sure they would. Everything was going according to plan. The food was spread out on a picnic blanket under the shade of a tree behind the Wishing Steps in Blarney Castle grounds.

He could have eaten a lot more, but then nuns were delicate and could not be expected to understand the appetite of a grown man doing a day's work. His stomach was not the only part of Ambrose's anatomy that would have welcomed attention at that point, but where to go? The amenities were too far away. Plenty of fields, of course, and hedges, but how to excuse yourself? Ambrose could not bring himself to say the words required, and since the two Sisters sat serenely making polite conversation with him throughout the lunch break, he had no opportunity to slip away.

By three o'clock in the afternoon the Sisters' serenity was intact but Ambrose was beginning to fidget.

'You'll be having no need of me for the moment, ladies,' he said, when they decided to pause for prayer at a small country chapel.

'Oh Mr O'Rourke,' cried Sister Theresa in a nasal Massachusetts twang , 'we should be honoured if you would share this small devotion with us.'

'And we know,' said Sister Mary Agnes, 'that you would welcome, as much as we do, a brief communication with our Lord.'

'Nothing,' said Ambrose, 'would give me more pleasure than to share a moment of worship with you.'

By five o'clock, posing in the cloisters of Bridgetown Abbey for yet another photograph to be taken back to America, Ambrose's discomfort had become acute. His collar was tightening, his face had reddened and the driving seat of the Ford was not at all as comfortable as he had thought it when they set out. All movement had become an agony, the bumps in the road a torment. The Sisters sat behind him, smiling benignly at the fields, glimpsed through the dense hedge. The rain had started again and lashed against the windscreen.

Sanctimonious biddies, don't they have bladders at all? he thought, as his knuckles whitened over the steering wheel. What kind of luck would a man have, to be saddled with such drones? A sensible woman like Margaret would understand when a man needed to duck behind a tree. Not even to wander off and leave him in peace for five minutes like normal people would. He wouldn't carry nuns again. 'A darling little place, is it?' I could tell you a thing or two about your quaint Celtic ancestors. They'd have him climbing the walls soon. The thought made him wince, and he gripped the wheel tighter.

'A wonderful day, Mr O'Rourke. My Sisters in Boston will be filled with envy when I tell them of the glories of the country and of your goodness and kindness.'

'The pleasure has been all mine,' gasped Ambrose, in a strangled voice. 'To have been able to show you a small portion of your history has done a wealth of good to my otherwise worthless soul.' He was sweating freely now.

'Yes, Ambrose, a lovely day,' said Sister Mary Agnes. 'Be sure to remember me to your dear wife. I'll be settling your account now, if I may.'

'No question of payment, Sister. I'm only thrilled to be of service to two charming handmaids of our Most Precious Lord.'

'You are too generous, Ambrose.'

The effusion of their protests and thanks, farewells and blessings delayed Ambrose for a further five minutes.

Finally he managed his goodbyes, reeled, buckling into the Ford and roared away at high speed.

'By God, Clancy,' said Ambrose later, having put his second pint on the slate at Ryan's pub. 'I tore all the rubber off the tyres getting away from that blasted convent. I swear to God, if I hadn't found two bricks to stand on, I would have drowned down there in that field, with the cows watching me.'

Clancy chafed his hands briskly, keeping his face turned towards the fire. 'Funny women, nuns,' he said.

The Honeymoon

It was the barking that woke him, although he did not realise it at first. As soon as he opened his eyes he turned towards his wife beside him, and smiled to himself. He still had not got used to having a wife, and such a wife. He had marvelled that a young, beautiful woman could have agreed to marry an old, crusty farmer like him. They had met at the races, and when she smiled and spoke to him he became dry-mouthed, and stammered like a boy. Theirs was a short, intense courtship, a heady meeting of minds and bodies. He still took pleasure from saying, 'I'll have to see what my wife thinks about that,' or 'I'd like you to meet my wife...'

He watched her for a few seconds as she slept until the barking started again. He knew immediately what it meant and leapt from the bed, hopping one legged to the window as he tried to pull his trousers on and see into the yard at the same time. The barking was high-pitched, yappy and excited, the voice of just one dog, but he knew it would not be on its own. Those damned mongrels of Helen's. Oh, Christ, he thought, not mongrels, of course, not with a drawerful of papers to go with them, wouldn't have the sense of mongrels. He turned to look at her still sleeping form and then as if feeling his look, she opened her eyes and smiled at him, and reached out her arm to him, inviting him back in to the bed.

'The dogs,' he said sharply, pulling on his boots, not trusting himself to say more.

'What,' said Helen, and then as she realised what he meant, 'Oh, God. No.'

'Oh, God, yes,' he said between his teeth.

'But, David,' she cried, 'it can't be. I'm sure I put them in the barn myself last night, just after dinner.' She was out of the bed now and straining to see from their bedroom window where the barking was coming from.

'Well, they're not there now,' he said and threw open the bedroom door and headed for the stairs.

'Wait for me. Oh, David, wait for me. You don't know for sure it's them. It could be strays wandering into the yard. Oh, wait. Let me come.'

'No. No, Helen, you stay there. It won't do you any good to come down now. I'll have to check and see what the damage is first.' He shouted this after him as he rushed out of the house, and headed for the nearest gate.

He could see two sheep on the ground near the back of the shed, their throats torn open, blood seeping onto their woollen shoulders. They were newly dead, no flies near them yet. The next one he found was still breathing, lying very still, too weak to cry out. She saw him approach, but made no move. Near the fence line was another, too far gone to save. The barking was coming from over the rise, and when he climbed the small hill, he saw Helen's dogs. Tinker, the male, had a sheep on the ground and was tearing at it, a deep grumbling issuing from his throat, but his tail wagging furiously. Belle, his sister was running backwards and forwards the length of the struggling sheep, barking hard, egging him on. At a shout from David she started, but then ran towards him, still barking and wagging her tail, welcoming him to join the fun. He grabbed her collar and shouted at Tinker who, unaware of his approach, continued to growl and gnash at the neck of the sheep. David pulled a piece of strong twine from his pocket and tied it to the bitch's collar and secured her to the fence. He looked around for a stick to hit the dog with to get him away from the sheep, but the short grass was bare. He ran forward and drew a kick on the dog, catching him in the side, under the ribs. The dog yelped and stopped for a moment to look around at David, giving him enough time to grab his collar and drag him to the fence and tie him up some feet away from Belle. Both dogs were panting fast and whining softly, their eyes bright, their tails wagging with pride. They lifted their smiling faces to him, anticipating praise.

David leaned on the gate to catch his breath, and shook his head, looking down at the sheep, which was now perfectly still. He did not look at the dogs or address them as they strained against their tether in an attempt to go to him. Slowly he turned his back and slowly he made his way back to the house.

Helen, partially dressed, had appeared in the kitchen yard, her hair dishevelled and her eyes wild. 'Say it isn't them,' she cried, but knew the answer from his bowed head and inability to look at her. He passed her without a word and entered the house, heading for the study, where the guns were kept. Helen ran after him, crying out, 'No, no, David. There must be something else we can do.' He ignored her, opened the gun cabinet and put the key in his pocket; grabbed a rifle and started to load. The sight of the barrel and rattle of cartridges made her flinch. She stood in the doorway breathless, taking in huge mouthfuls of air.

'Oh, David, you can't,' she gasped, 'this is all wrong. There must be another way.' Her husband ignored her and continued to check the rifle.

'I can't stand this. There must be something else we can do,' she said to the back of his head. He did not move, or turn, or give any indication of having heard her. She raised her voice, 'I said...'

'I heard what you said, dammit, I'm not deaf,' he said, without turning. Then his shoulders sagged and he turned towards her, 'I'm sorry Helen, but you know this is the third time they have caused havoc in a month. We have had this conversation twice before. I made it perfectly clear what would happen if those ridiculous animals got loose among the sheep. You must understand. This is not a stroll in the park with your pets in their fancy collars on a Sunday morning. This is the country. This is my farm, passed down through generations. These sheep and cows are my livelihood. If the dogs can't be controlled then I'm sorry, but they have to go. If I don't do it someone else will. What if they spooked the horses or stampeded the cattle? First it was the chickens they chased and killed; then they harassed George's prize bull. What excuse would you like me to make to him if the bull charged and damaged itself, do you have any idea what that animal is worth??' When she did not reply, he said, 'we can't afford incidents like this. They've killed five sheep his time, if not more.'

She balled her handkerchief and scrubbed it across her face. She was red and weeping, her breath rasping. 'Is that all you think about, money?' she cried.

He sighed and put the gun down carefully on the table. He reached for her hand and sat on the couch and pulled her down next to him. He took a deep breath. He reminded himself that Helen was a city girl, that her inexperience of country life he had once found charming, her ignorance, endearing. 'Are you sure you locked them up last night?' he asked gently. She shook her head, not daring to look up from the floor, and mumbled, 'I forgot,' and then rushed on, ' But they wouldn't have meant any harm. They would have thought it was a game.'

'Darling girl,' he said, 'this is not a game. It's our life and our living. We have to protect it.'

'You've got dogs,' she cried, jumping up from the seat.

'They're working dogs, Helen, as well you know, and if they killed sheep I would shoot them too.'

'I can't believe that you could be so cold, so cruel.' She cried.

'And I can't believe that you could be so stupid,' he roared, jumping to his feet. 'How the hell hard is it to lock two stupid mutts into the barn for the night?'

He strode to the table and picked up the rifle. 'I won't let you,' she shouted, grabbing his arm and trying to grapple the weapon from his grasp. The report deafened them both to the sound of breaking glass, but they stopped struggling and stood completely still, staring at each other in shock for long seconds. David recovered first. 'You bloody little fool,' he cried, 'you could have killed one of us. Let me go.' And he shook her hand free. 'Go back to the bedroom,' he ordered, knowing that she could not see where he was going from that side of the house. When she made no effort to move, he roughly pushed her towards the door. 'Go back to the bedroom, I said. Do you hear me? Go.'

Helen looked vacantly at the shattered window, and then down at her bare feet, noticing for the first time that she had grazed her foot on the gravel path and a trickle of blood was staining the carpet. She felt suddenly cold and pulled her gown around her. When she looked up into his face, she shuddered slightly, turned gradually and walked out of the door into the hallway towards the stairs.

As she leaned out of the bedroom window she tried to see which direction her husband was heading, but could see only a light breeze rippling across the orchard and small clouds scudding over the hill. She could hear birdsong over to her left and a plaintive mooing in the distance. As she pulled her gown tighter around her shoulders she heard the crack of the pistol shot, once, twice, then silence.

PUSH

'YOU CAN PUSH now, if you like,' said Tom.

'No, I can't. I'm not ready yet,' she replied and he could hear her panting.

'OK, babe, take your time,' he said trying to muffle a yawn.

'Oh, dear, you poor thing. You're tired,' she said,' not holding you up am I?'

'Of course not,' he said in the conciliatory voice he had suddenly perfected, 'you know I'd do it for you if I could.'

'Ok, let's not start that 'It's all your own fault, you should take more care' stuff again, shall we? '

'Take your time, calm your breathing and push when you're ready,' he intoned this mantra in a bored monotone.

'I'm thirsty,' she said, and he jumped up from his seat and rummaged in his bag for a bottle of water.

'You're sweating,' he said and clumsily tried to wipe her forehead with his handkerchief. She brushed him away, turning her head in irritation.

'It's too late to go back now,' he said quietly, from a safe distance.

'Is that all you've got?' she said, 'platitudes?'

He slumped back into his seat and did not answer; this was no a time for argument. He took a couple of deep breaths, to calm down, and then smiled to himself. They'd laugh about this together later.

She called to him softly and he lurched awkwardly to her side.

'I'm sorry,' she whispered, her faltering hand reaching for his, 'You're right and I should have listened to you. It's just so hard. I don't think I'm strong enough, and it hurts.' She squeezed his hand. Then, smiling, 'I'll be all right, really. I'm ready now,' and took a shaky breath.

'Good for you,' he said and squeezed her hand again.

Then he dashed back to his seat, released the handbrake and yelled, 'OK, push.'

Fruit and Nut

For a second she looked frightened as if she was going to cry, but she recovered her composure immediately. No sigh of weakness must be shown. A predator like Ralph would enjoy any hint of panic. She knew that much from her psychology lectures the previous year. She had studied Abnormal Psychology with Professor Watts, a brilliant man. He had revealed to her the reasons for so much of her husband's strange behaviour. She had recommended the course to everyone, even Ralph. My God, even Ralph. What would he think if he were in the lecture hall and Professor Watts was describing sociopathic behaviour? Would he think, 'Oh yeah, so that's what I am.'

Ralph came towards her with the tray. His head was cocked on one side and he had a little smile on his face. She closed her eyes so that she did not have to look at him.

'Here's some nice breakfast for you,' he said in his soft voice. 'You'd like some muesli wouldn't you, and I've made coffee. Kenyan, your favourite, brewed just the way you like it.'

His tone terrified her, but he mustn't know. She knew that the gentle voice he affected when talking to her, and only to her, was part of the plan to make her think she was losing her mind. She could hear him sometimes from down below shouting at the housekeeper and banging doors. She knew well how impatient and irritable he could be with his own mother, who absolutely idolised him.

He placed the tray on the bedside table and stood back with his hands folded looking at her. 'This won't do at all Clare,' he said, 'You're only going to make yourself ill and that's no help to anyone.' And then he left the room. Clare did not know whether to be relieved that he had gone or apprehensive about what he would do next. The fact that he did not abuse or threaten her made her somehow more frightened than less.

His mother had painfully climbed the stairs early this morning to talk to her, to try to make her 'see sense', as she put it. 'But, darling, we only want what's best for you. Why won't you dress and have lunch with us on the verandah? It's such a beautiful day and the garden is glorious.'

'Because I am forbidden to leave this room, forbidden do you hear me, by your son.'

'But how can that be, dear? The door isn't locked, there is no one guarding your door to stop you from coming out. You're just a little overwrought. It's been so hard for you, losing the baby. I understand that, of course I do. You've had an absolutely beastly time. But you know, darling, Ralph is devastated too. I know you must give up you dream of being a mother, but Ralph, poor Ralph was yearning to be a father, and he has been so brave, trying to come to terms with it.'

'Your beastly son doesn't care about anything except my money,' Clare shouted and then lay back on the pillows exhausted.

'Oh, but where do you get these terrible notions from?' wailed her mother in law. 'He adores you. How can you not see that? He's broken hearted about the baby and just crushed that you have drawn away from him.'

'You'll have to go now. I've got a headache,' said Clare, and turned her back. She could see Ralph's mother reflected in the dressing table mirror and felt vaguely sorry for the older woman as she stood there wringing her hands.

When she was alone again, Clare turned on her side on the bed and drew her knees up until she was in a foetal position. She gazed idly around the room at the furniture. She suddenly spotted that one of the knobs on the chest of drawers was different from the other seven. Remarkable, she thought, absolutely remarkable. I've slept in this room since I've been married and I never, ever noticed that before. She sat up in the bed, her eyes shining with curiosity and rushed over to the chest of drawers to examine the errant knob. When she opened the drawer and looked at the back of the knob she could see that the whole fitting was completely different from the others. One must have broken and been replaced with something similar, such a good match that she, who flattered herself that on her excellent powers of observation, had not seen it until now. Now that her attention had been drawn to the vagaries of the fittings on the furniture she began to examine minutely every hinge, handle and button around the room. To her disappointment this did not take long, and she found no more irregularities to attract her attention.

When she heard Ralph's step on the stair, she quickly got back into bed with her hands clasped tightly to her chest. When he came into the room, she closed her eyes tight. Important not to make eye contact or he would try to bully her again.

Ralph sighed gently when he saw the untouched breakfast tray. 'You must eat something, Clare. You'll make yourself ill if you don't let me take care of you.'

'Turn me into a raving lunatic, you mean. Wouldn't that be handy? You could get power of attorney and have me carted off. Wouldn't you have fun, then, though, you and your floozy?' she shot at him without moving and without opening her eyes. She heard him softly approach the bed, she could hear him breathing calmly and regularly and could smell the expensive cologne she had bought him, last year, for no other reason except that she loved him. She groaned aloud when she thought of that time in the Seychelles when everything was wonderful.

He heard her groan and he leaned forward to touch her arm, 'I know,' he started, and she leapt up in the bed, pushed his hand angrily away and pulled the bedclothes up to her chin. 'Don't touch me.' She hissed at him.

'I only want to help, Clare. You know you can trust me.' She gave a short, high shrill laugh.

'Trust?' she cried, 'trust you?'

'Try to keep your voice down. You'll frighten my mother. God knows she's distressed enough by all this.' He said.

'Why is she here, then?' Clare asked, 'Is she your alibi for when you do away with me and she can tell everyone what a little painted sepulchre her darling boy was, putting up with his mad wife? She doesn't know you half as well as she thinks she does, does she Ralph, my darling husband?' His grip on the tray tightened perceptibly, but he merely said, in his tired, soft voice. 'I'll take the tray away, you might feel like a bite of lunch later.'

Of course, she knew why Ralph served her himself, he would not let anyone else near her in case they helped her to escape. She did not know if he prepared the food himself so she could not be sure that he had not tampered with it in some way. Judging by the way things were arranged on the tray Mrs Parker, the cook, must have helped him with it. Ralph would never have thought to put the correct spoon out for the marmalade, or served the butter curled.

She listened to his steps receding down the stairs, and then left the bed. She drew the bedside chair over to the fitted wardrobe, climbed up, slid back the door and took out a large biscuit tin. She sat on the chair, opened the tin and took out a handful of mixed fruit and nuts and shovelled them roughly into her mouth. She had read that when Dervla Murphy travelled in Russia she took a kilo of mixed raisins and peanuts as sufficient for a five-day train trip, where she would be mostly inactive. On a whim Clare had bought the same, but it had to last her a lot more than five days and her supplies were running low. When she put the tin away, she went to the en suite and cleaned her teeth. Ralph mustn't know that she had anything to eat. But how would she get more, since she couldn't leave the bedroom let alone the house? She looked out of the window. The orchard was spread before her, which had been her delight along with the walled garden at the rear of the house. She had inherited this house when her parents died, along with the business and her grandfather's fortune. She had met Ralph at the office and they had moved into this house when they got married.

'Our rural idyll', he had called it when he made her sell the house in town. She soon understood why he wanted her isolated from all her friends. Now she wished she had close neighbours so that she could attract their attention and be rescued. She had previously thought to write a note to Mrs Parker begging for help, and hide it under the saucer of her tray. But she knew this would do no good. That swine had the whole place convinced she was out of her mind, so Mrs Parker would probably shake her head sadly over such a plea and immediately show it to Ralph. Or else he would find it and punish her.

She jumped up and raised the foot of the mattress to retrieve her journal. She had started documenting everything that went on and needed to find a better hiding place for the book. She pulled out the black and red notebook. It was half filled with her cramped handwriting and across the front page in large staggered letters she had written, 'To be passed to my solicitor in the event of my sudden death.' It was important that Ralph did not get hold of this document because he would destroy it and all her suffering would be for nothing. She couldn't bear to think that he would escape the punishment he deserved.

She frantically scanned the room as she had done so often before looking for a hiding place that he would not find, but that someone else would. My God, would they think her mad even after he had killed her? There was nowhere. She walked the room in circles, agitatedly tearing at her fingernails and pulling at the hair that now hung into her eyes in greasy tendrils. She opened her chest of drawers, where she had examined the knobs previously, making a point of opening the drawer with the alteration. She pulled out underwear, socks, tights, and a negligee that Ralph had bought her, still in the wrapper. Suddenly she stopped perfectly still. The plastic wrapper. She hurriedly but carefully took the negligee out of its wrapper and put the book inside the plastic. Perfect. She sealed it back up and rushed into the en suite and put the precious package inside the cistern. She laughed out loud. Why hadn't she thought of that before? She quickly quieted herself. What if they should hear her downstairs? She hastened back into the bedroom in time to hear the kitchen door on the other side of the house closing. That would be Mrs Parker going home, but then she heard a car door. Surely Ralph hadn't gone out and left her here alone? Ah no, his mother was still there. Would she stop me leaving the house? Then she could hear voices. She went to the window and strained to hear. Ralph and his mother, and then a car door again. Were they all gone? But then she heard the car pull away and Ralph calling out, and then the slam as he came back into the house.

Clare looked frantically around the room. They were the only ones left. Where could she hide? She raced to the door and flung it open, only to see her husband climbing the stairs. When he saw her at the door, he gave her that familiar tired smile, and as he advanced she backed into the bedroom and raced to the sanctuary of the bed.

'My, my,' he said, as he came in, 'all the way to the door eh?' She didn't reply but kept her eyes on his every movement. He turned, and from his right hand pocket produced a key, turned it in the lock of the door and returned it to his pocket. He had a bottle of mineral water in his other hand, which he placed on the bedside table. From his left hand pocket he took a large bottle of what she recognised as the sleeping pills her doctor had prescribed but she had refused to take.

Still smiling his small, private smile, Ralph sat on the foot of the bed facing his wife. 'Now, my dear, at last we have the house all to ourselves. And I have a feast here for you that you will not be able to refuse.'

Whispering

It was early in the morning as I made my slow way towards the shops. The main street shone with a bright patina of rain that hurt my eyes. I trudged, forcing every step, up the Main Street, dragging my feet in the old slippers I normally only wore around the house but had forgotten to change out of. My mother used to say, 'Pick your feet, up and stop scuffling. You're slouching around like an old man.' As a child I could run up this street on the way to school if I had messages to get, and home across the field in the evening, impatient to throw down the satchel and head for the river. Now my leaden feet resisted speed and the impatience had seeped out of me, like water percolating through moss. By the time I got to the chemist the rain was beginning to find ways to creep down the back of my neck.

'Take an umbrella,' Tom had shouted from the living room, as I was putting on my coat.

'Yes, dear,' I said, but I forgot and left the umbrella in the old green and red chipped pottery vase that stood in the corner of the hallway, and had been used for an umbrella stand since before Daddy died. At least I tried to answer him, but I knew he would not hear me above the roar of the television. He spent most his time, these days, either reading the paper, chatting to friends who called, or watching old war films. Since he started to lose his hearing, the house had echoed with the sound of constant enemy bombardment.

* * *

I am standing, knee deep in the river with my sisters, at the back of our house. We are supposed to be fishing, but we have never caught anything. We are not allowed to swim, my mother says we'll drown, so we stand in the water holding a stick with a piece of string and a bent safety pin on the end, pretending to fish, but really we are trying to decide what kind of man we would like to marry. Handsome and rich we have ticked off our list, but are not sure where to go from there. We decide to get hold of one of those magazines that tell you all about men. Soon it will be time to get out of the water and dry our legs, but we don't hurry. There's a dragonfly right in front of me skimming the water's surface.

* * *

The chemist was not open yet; I was ten minutes early. I stood in the doorway trying to avoid the rain, keeping my head down, as if that would make me invisible.

'Hello Mary. How's Tom?' Four different people asked me this while I waited the long minutes it took for the girl arrive, turn the 'Closed' sign round and unlock the door. I gave the usual array of answers, 'Great now, thank God,' or 'much better now he has the new tablets,' or 'on the mend now, please God.'

The answer was always the same, 'you're lucky to have him all the same. A grand fellow.'

'He is that,' I replied and cemented a smile across my face so false that I expected them to flinch, but they were gone, rushing through the soaking drizzle to whatever important place they were going.

* * *

I'm standing just inside the door, near a pillar, wishing I could hide behind it. My two sisters are in front of me giggling with a couple of the lads from out of town. The boys have come from the pub and are full of bravado. My sisters are older than me, and stick close together like they never would at home. One of the boys looks over at me and whispers something to his pal, and then they both look at me, brazen. I want the floor to open up and swallow me. I want to run out of the dancehall, but I am unable to move. My sisters turn to look at me and I hear one of them say to the boys. 'Oh, she's all right. She's just shy.' Then they all step aside as a tall dark haired boy, no not a boy, he's a man, parts the group and comes up to me.

'Would you like to dance?' he asks in a soft melodious voice. I blush and stutter, 'Oh, yes, please.' And he leads me on to the floor.

'My name's Tom,' he whispers into my hair.

* * *

Mr Flynn, the pharmacist, quizzed me about Tom's medication. Was he taking the tablets according to the instructions? Was the physiotherapist still calling twice a week? I had been nursing my sick husband for more years that I cared to remember, and still the doctor and the nurse and the chemist quizzed me closely abut my precious charge. 'Yes,' I said in a small, stiff voice, 'everything is going along as well as can be expected.'

Mr Flynn laughed his high, tinny laugh and said, 'Got to look after our favourite referee, haven't we? The boys are waiting for him to get back on the pitch. Tell him we'll be thinking of him on Saturday at the match.'

'I will indeed, he'll be delighted. Not as delighted as he'd be to be out there with you all, but pleased to be thought of all the same.'

'Ah, sure, he's a great fellow,' said Mr Flynn.

'He is that,' I said, and showed him my plastered-on smile.

When I got home, Tom was waiting for his coffee and the paper. 'What took you so long, for Christ's sake?'

'The chemist wasn't open yet.'

'More fool you for going out too early, and look at you. I told you to take an umbrella, but no, you know everything better than I do.'

'It was only a shower, Tom,' I said, straightening his pillows, and trying to plump them up a bit. He needed new pillows, these were flat and stained under the pillowslips and I was ashamed when the doctor came, but Tom refused to part with them. 'I'm not made of money, woman, whatever you might think,' he roared when I mentioned it. 'It's my legs that won't work, not my brain. Wouldn't you love it now if I gave you a fistful of notes that you could swan around town picking up any old gewgaw that took you fancy? For pity sake, stop poking at me,' he said, and pushed me so roughly that I stumbled into the corner of the small table but managed to save myself from falling.

'That's right,' he said, 'throw yourself down and then you can go running to one of your idiot sisters and tell her I hit you. At least your mother had the sense to send you scuttling back when you ran blubbering to her.' He lay back on the pillows and took a deep breath. Then he turned and said in a slow, patient voice. 'Now, you are supposed to get my coffee. Think you can manage that?' Without answering I went to the kitchen to make the coffee, and put his favourite, a vanilla slice that I had just got fresh from the baker, on the tray for his mid morning snack.

* * *

I'm standing at the sink, looking out of the kitchen window at what's left of the roses. They badly need pruning, but I never seem to have time. The thorns on the pink ones are particularly vicious, dozens of them on the one stem, there's no pleasure in trying to cut them to put in a vase. They used to be Tom's pride and joy, but he can't bear to look at them now. I can feel my heart thumping in my chest, pushing the blood through my sluggish arteries. It's not right that I should be so tired. I only have Tom to look after, imagine if I had a house full of children. I'd be dead on my feet. Next time I take Tom to the doctor, I'll ask him for something to give me a bit of energy, a bit of a boost. That's what I need, a tonic.

* * *

As I waited for the kettle to boil I pushed sheets and pillowslips into the washing machine, put one heaped scoop of powder into the little drawer and closed it; turned the knob to 'whites only'; the water would be nice and hot and the linen lovely and clean and fresh. I pulled the button to start the wash quickly, guiltily. Tom said we didn't need to have the water so hot, it cost a fortune and the clothes were no different, but I always liked to think they were better for a hot wash, and that he would be more comfortable in fresh smelling, ironed sheets.

As I carried the tray in to Tom, the doorbell went. I put the tray down to answer the door. The caller was a friend of Tom's from the GAA.

'Come in Jerry,' Tom called from the living room, 'great to see you. A man could go mad sitting all day looking at the goggle box and no one to talk to, but the lads are great to pop in. I'm kept well up to date. Get another cup there for Jerry.'

* * *

I am sitting in the bedroom on a straight-backed chair, the Daily Mirror on my lap. I don't like the Daily Mirror but it is the only newspaper that Tom will allow inside the door. I have the small satisfaction of burning yesterday's paper in the grate every morning to light the fire.

I suddenly realise that I am sliding off the chair. I must have drifted off to sleep while I was doing the crossword. I can't take to that Suduko. I have tried but can't find the energy to care whether I get it out or not. Words, though, are a different matter. When I have a free moment I like to read. I am reading a novel by Niall Tobin just now that I got from the library. Tom doesn't like me to read, thinks novels are a waste of time when I could be doing something useful. I jump to my feet and rush to the kitchen to look at the clock and then listen for sounds from the living room. All's well, they are still talking. I ease the tension out of my shoulders; he doesn't need anything yet.

* * *

The door slammed as Jerry left. When I went back into Tom, he looked relaxed and had a slight smile on his face. When he saw me the smile faded and he said, 'Bring me my glasses from wherever you've put them.'

I handed him his glasses, which were perched on the arm of his chair, and I said, knowing that he was fond of fish, 'I was thinking of steaming a bit of haddock for your dinner. Would that be nice?'

'Do what you like,' he said, picking up the newspaper and turning to the back page, 'you'll probably ruin it anyway, whatever it is.'

* * *

I'm lying on the floor in the kitchen. I can see the window of the washing machine and the sheets pushing their suds at the porthole, but I'm not able to hear the motor, only a kind of whooshing sound. I must get up; it will be time for Tom's bath soon, but I'm lying on my arm and I can't seem to shift it to push myself up. Is that Tom, calling me? His voice sounds like it's coming from a long way off. It's only a soft whisper in my ear.

REYNARD THE FOX

'WHY DO THEY call you Ray if your real name is George?' Lenny was looking at the newspaper cutting he had just pulled out of the biscuit tin on the shelf near the bunks.

Ray snatched the tin from him, and raised his fist as if he was going to hit him. Lenny shrank back. 'Sorry Ray, I didn't know it was private. I was just looking to see if you had a pen.'

'Well, don't go poking around where you're not wanted, right?' snarled Ray. 'A man can't even have a thought in this rotten dump without everyone wanting to know about it.' He roughly shoved the tin under the flat pillow on his bunk although up until then it had been sitting on the shelf the whole time he and Lenny had shared a cell. 'If I want you to know something, I'll tell you. OK? Don't go sneaking around in my things.'

Lenny climbed onto the top bunk and lay flat on his back looking at the ceiling. He knew there was no point arguing with Ray when he was in this mood, but he'd come round. He and Ray had been sharing this cell for over a year now, and knew each other's moods. Ray thought of himself as a hard man, but Lenny was a lot younger and fitter. And anyway, Ray needed him.

When Lenny first arrived at the prison and was put in a cell with Ray he tried to talk to him, but Ray ignored him for days, merely indicating by a nod of his head that Lenny was to take the top bunk. The younger man had never been in jail before which suited Ray fine. All he had to do was keep him in his place and life would go on without any hiccups. Lenny's tentative enquiry, 'What you in for then?' was treated with a look of silent scorn.

'I'm in for...' Lenny started to say, but Ray batted away this information with a wave of his nicotine stained fingers. 'We all know what you're in for, chum,' he said and that ended the conversation until about half way through the second week.

One day when Lenny came back from the shower and was combing his hair at the small cracked mirror on the wall, Ray said, 'What happened to your stash then?' Lenny started at the sound of his voice, and just turned and stared at him, not knowing how he could avoid answering without getting his head kicked in. He put the comb down carefully and turned back to the mirror. Checking his chin to make sure he hadn't nicked himself shaving, he said, 'Wouldn't you like to know?'

Ray threw back his head and laughed a hoarse, crowing laugh that ended in a coughing fit. 'Good answer, young'un,' he croaked and went back to reading his paper.

After that Ray took him under his wing and showed him how to get round the place, who to trust (no one), who to avoid, and which wardens would bend the rules for you, if you slipped them a bribe. Lenny couldn't believe the drugs and money that got in on visiting day, but most of their perks came in via a sympathetic or greedy warder, and that's how Ray got the mobile phone. After that, things started to happen, more quickly than Lenny could follow, but exciting all the same. Ray let him use the phone to ring his girlfriend whenever he liked. He could have used the phone in the hall, but they were only allowed one call, one day a week.

Lenny and his brother Paul had pulled an armed robbery at the shoe factory and would have got away with it too, if the stolen plates hadn't fallen off the back of Lenny's car. Paul was only seventeen and by the time the police traced the car, Paul had scarpered with the money and Lenny took the rap, deciding to keep his little brother out of it. Nobody believed him when he said he had done the robbery on his own, but the CCTV was broken and the guard had concussion and could not remember anything, so the police could not prove Paul was involved. The brothers had agreed to hide the payroll they had stolen and leave it for a year not to arouse suspicion, but Paul was just a lad with no sense, and Lenny was scared the money would be too much temptation for a headstrong teenager.

Once Ray had started talking there was no stopping him. He had worked out this foolproof way of escaping, he said. 'I'm not sitting here for the next twenty years,' he said.

'Twenty years?' said Lenny, 'why what did you do?'

'They reckon I killed a man,' said Ray, 'but I didn't. I was stitched up. I want to get out of here and clear my name.'

'Yeah,' said Lenny, 'course you do.'

The next day, Lenny asked Ray, 'How would we do it?'

'Do what?'

'Escape. I want to go with you. We could do it together. I could help.' He perched on the edge of the bunk watching Ray's every move as he slowly rolled a cigarette.

'No way sonny,' scoffed Ray. 'I'm going on my own. Don't want any snot nosed boy hanging off my coat tails when I get over the wall.'

'Come on Ray,' Lenny pleaded, and Ray let him plead for a week before he finally gave in and said, 'Alright, alright, you're driving me mad with your nagging. Worse than an old woman. You can come too, OK, but we'll need money. I'd have been long gone if I'd had the money for the bribes, and then there's money for when I'm on the outside.'

'Well, there you go then,' said Lenny, leaning back in his chair and glancing around the recreation hall to make sure nobody was listening. They were playing gin rummy and when Lenny leaned forward again, he laid his hand down, and said, 'Full house, Ray, me old mate. I'm on a winning streak.'

The plan was for them both to get jobs in the laundry. With Ray's help Lenny would smuggle some of his share of the robbery in to bribe the guard to look the other way when the laundry van came. The two fugitives would then hide in the laundry hampers and be wheeled out to the van as sweet as you please.

'And then,' explained Ray, 'when it pulls up at the hospital to deliver the sheets and stuff, we jump out and hoof it.'

After a while Ray got up and put the tin back on the shelf where it always sat and said, 'It's a nickname, on account of me being a bit on the clever side. Called after Reynard the fox from folklore.'

'Never heard of him,' said Lenny, losing interest.

'The fox,' Ray went on, ' is said to be good at planning and thinking ahead. Cunning some might say, but I like to work things out, and know where I'm headed.'

'Wasn't it the fox that got done over by the three little pigs?' asked Lenny.

'No, mate,' said Ray, smirking to himself 'that was a wolf. A fox wouldn't have fallen for their stupid tricks. He'd have had a fine full belly.'

Ray did all the scheming and Lenny provided all the money. The deal was that Ray would do the planning and organising and Lenny would take him to the hoard and they would share it out and then split up.

'What about Paul?' asked Lenny.

'Oh, yeah, well obviously it'll be a three way cut but in the meantime don't say a word. Tell no one,' said Ray, 'trust me, the fewer people involved the safer it will be for both of us. You can call him up and give him his share when we've got well away.'

The escape went without a hitch. They could hardly stop from laughing in the back of the laundry van. 'Just as well, it's clean washing,' whispered Lenny through the gaps in the wicker hamper, 'wouldn't want to be doing a *dirty deed*.' And the two of them stifled giggles like a pair of schoolboys. There were wardsmen's uniforms in the van and a couple of blue cotton jackets, so they quickly got changed and stuffed their prison garb into the bottom of one of the hampers. The van pulled up outside the hospital, and the two fugitives jumped down and casually walked through the hospital entrance and out the back door, wheeling an empty stretcher they spotted in the corridor, then they dumped it in the car park like a shopping trolley. A couple of minutes later Lenny had started one of the parked cars and they drove sedately across town, careful not to attract attention, to the warehouse where the money was hidden.

Lenny's hands were sweating as he hauled up the floorboards and groped around for the coal bag they had stuffed the money into. He made a small satisfied grunt when his fingers found the bag, and gently pulled it up onto the floor of one of the offices in the abandoned warehouse. He turned around, smiling, and looked into the barrel of a pistol that Ray was pointing at his head.

'What the hell are you doing, Ray?' he said, and Ray just motioned him with the gun to move away from the money. Lenny backed away and put his hands out to his side.

'I think I might have all of that, thanks, Lenny,' said Ray, with a chuckle, and he pulled the trigger. The tinny click that followed echoed in the silent room, and he looked down in disbelief at the gun in his hand, as Lenny sprang forward and punched him hard in the face. The gun went skittering across the floor and Ray landed heavily against an upturned desk.

Lenny pushed him to the floor and sat on the older man's chest so that he could not move. 'You didn't think I was going to let you carry that thing around loaded, did you?' he asked Ray, and pulled rope from his pocket to secure Ray's wrists and ankles to the legs of the desk. 'They should have called you after the leopard, old man. You've never changed your spots have you? Easier to kill the second time is it Ray?'

'Christ Lenny,' gasped Ray, 'you've got it all wrong. I wasn't going to shoot you. The gun went off in my hand, I swear.'

Lenny cuffed him sharply across the head, 'Shut up, Ray. The jig's up,' and he reached inside the shackled man's jacket and took out the mobile phone. 'I'll have this too, thanks,' he said, adding, 'did I tell you my girlfriend dumped me months ago? But I've been having some lovely little chats with my brother.' He quickly dialled a number. 'Yeah,' he said into the phone, 'all done here, bring the van round the front. No, just me.'

Ray stared at him, eyes widening in terror. 'You can't leave me here, Lenny. For the love of God, son, don't leave me here. They'll never find me,' and his eyes darted around the room as if he could already see rats advancing towards him.

'I'll kill you, you little punk,' snarled Ray.

'Don't think so, old-timer,' laughed Lenny, 'you've already missed your chance for that. By the time you're all tucked up cosy back in your little cell, this little piggy will be long gone. Not to worry, Reynard, I'm no killer. As soon as Paul gets here I'm off and when we're far, far away, I'll get a message to the governor and tell him where to pick you up.'

When I'm a man

When I'm a man
I'm gonna live in the bush
On a property, and raise sheep,
Or cattle or caulies – or something.
I'll have a white ute, a one tonner
To take to town on a Friday
With a bale in the back and wire and string.
And a bloody great spotlights for rabitting.
And a shotgun with plenty of ammo.

Pa'll give me my own blue heeler,
Mean as buggery,
Built like a brick dunny.

And he can thrash around in the back
Barking his damn, fool head off,
As we rattle across the paddocks
Flinging empty tinnies at the bunnies.

That Bitch

'That bitch wants to come to my graduation,' said Fiona, critically examining the wine glasses for smears. When she was satisfied, she laid the glasses on the table and brought the bottle of wine from the kitchen. 'Red with quiche, do you mind, it's all I've got?'

'Lovely,' said Helen, making an ungainly attempt to move forward on the overstuffed couch that doubled as a spare bed in the lounge room. 'I thought you wanted your mother to come, so that you could flaunt your 'finest hour' in front of her.'

'I'll have to put up with her, I suppose, though I don't think the penniless, middle aged, divorced daughter's academic success will go down quite as well as the younger, more beautiful daughter's barrister husband, high cheek bones and Jacuzzi.' Fiona laughed loudly to cover the tremble in her voice. 'The fact that I'm happy as a clam and 'beautiful, successful, younger daughter' is in therapy is neither here nor there as far as my dear Mama is concerned.'

'How is Angela?' said Helen, of the sister whom she had never met. She and Fiona had met at the university where she was impressed with the other's cool, intelligent appraisal of texts and authors that Helen herself sometimes struggled with.

'God knows,' said Fiona, 'I haven't seen any of the family for months. They seem to be intimidated by their 'scholarly' sister. Isn't that a hoot? I suppose they think that anyone who can still walk and talk at the same time, as she totters towards her dotage is some kind of biological phenomenon. My brother insists on referring to my doctorate as 'your little hobby" She threw herself back dramatically in her armchair, her melodious laugh filling the small room. She had, invested in coaching to rid her voice of any hint of Australian twang, and now spoke in deep, languid tones that reminded Helen of warm cream.

Clutching her favourite cat with one hand, and waving the other arm dramatically in the air, Fiona cried, 'Thank God, anyway, that I was spared the horror of taking after my mother, self centred snob that she is.' Her tabby, Marquis, wriggled free and Fiona went on, 'No,' she said, casually dropping broken crusts of burned-edged quiche onto two small plates, ' what really gives me the horrors is that if I let her come to the graduation, she'll want to stay here. Not that she can't afford a hotel, or that I want her here, or even that *she* wants to be here. No, she just wants to discombobulate me for a few days, (isn't that a wonderful word?) and poke around the house, sneering and criticising – offering 'tentative' little suggestions like,' and she leaned backwards waving a pretend cigarette holder, 'I wonder, darling, if blue walls would go better with those curtains than that strange shade of orange.' She never does anything but whine. When I first got this place, and I'm sure I've bored you to sobs before with this little tale – she came to see it, wanting to know where her money had gone, no doubt. She raced through the place like a dervish and then sniffed and said, 'Could do with a few pot plants, don't you think? I ask you.' Fiona dashed to the kitchen and brought back a bowl of salad and a small bone china jug filled with balsamic dressing.

'I suppose giving you the deposit for the house redeems her somewhat,' said Helen, pulling lettuce and tomato out of the bowl with her own fork.

'I'm sure she thinks so,' said Fiona, 'but she managed to bitch for months first about how I'd frittered away my divorce settlement, such as it was. As if I didn't desperately need a good holiday after my ghastly husband ran off with that hussy next door. And despite what she might think, I had no intention of barrelling around the town in that old banger, waiting for it to fall to bits. No, I needed a decent car, and I got one.' Her artist husband had not only disappeared with another woman, but had taken most of his meagre assets with him, leaving her a few paintings to sell.

The two friends ate silently for a few minutes, to the muffled sound of Mozart's clarinet concerto. Marquis had returned, and Fiona sat clutching him to her breast. She leaned back with her eyes closed, her titian hair spread out on the back of the chair, exactly matched by the silk scarf at her throat. 'Isn't Amadeus just divine?' she breathed.

Helen shifted awkwardly on the sagging couch, knowing that if she needed to get up she would have to roll sideways almost on to the floor to get enough leverage to rise. It had been dragged kicking and screaming from the bean-bagged seventies, with no pretensions of being a normal seat. Fiona said it reminded her of her misspent youth, and she couldn't bear to part with it. As she reached for her glass the couch swayed dangerously, and Fiona suddenly opened her eyes and laughed.

'Terrible bloody thing, isn't it? That's why I always sit here. Mother will insist on multiple cushions before she deigns to sit down. Maybe I should make her sleep on it.'

'Well,' said Helen, straightening up, 'I'm sure she is very proud that you got your doctorate after all your years of slaving away over poor, mad Virginia Woolf.'

'If she is, she does a damn good job of hiding it.' She frowned into her merlot.

'Oh, well,' said Helen. She was anxiously waiting for feedback from her friend on the latest essay before she handed it in. Despite getting high grades and positive comments from her tutor for all her work so far, she lacked courage and confidence, and looked to her successful, highly literate friend for encouragement. She made one last stab at the perennial issue of Fiona's mother, ' It's only for a few days I guess, and she will doubtless bring you extravagant presents, as she always does,' hoping to close the topic and finally bring up the subject of her essay.

'I don't know why,' her husband had said to her, yet again, that afternoon before she left the house, 'you put up with that dreadful woman. She does no better than you academically and you treat her like some sort of guru.' Although she defended her friend and insisted that theirs was an equal exchange of ideas and encouragement, his comments were secretly quite gratifying to Helen. She had initially been nervous about introducing him to Fiona lest he be smitten by her beauty and brilliance. Not that she didn't trust him, of course, but Fiona, by her own admission, appeared to have a giddying affect on 'mere menfolk', as she called them.

'Oh, look, that's enough about me, for God's sake, and my blasted mother,' cried Fiona as the music faded. She sat back cross-legged in the armchair, her tiny knees barely reaching the arms. 'What about you? How's that sweet, dependable husband of yours? And when on earth are you going to buy some paint to tart up that pokey little box you're living in? Oh, and by the way, I read your essay. Enthralling, my dear, you'll knock 'em dead. Wait, Leonard Cohen, that's what we need now, dear Leonard,' and she sprang up flinging Marquis aside.

SEEING SOMEONE

THE BEDROOM was large and bright, with sunlight and air bustling in from the east. The walls had been painted in a matt finish, in what was called 'Parisian Cream' on the colour chart but on the walls, looked more like the underside of a wild mushroom. It worked surprisingly well, giving the room a warmth and intimacy missing from the light woodwork and functional lines of the furniture and the futuristic lamps. The windows were draped in gauze coloured hangings that leaned away from the breeze. The large bed was neatly made, corners tucked in, sheet folded down evenly over the top of an off white counterpane. The only splatter of colour in the room came from a bowl of tulips, their scarlet petals lush and shocking, standing defiantly against the light gust that puffed at them. The austerity of the room was relieved by the flowers and by a blonde girl who stood near the foot of the bed with her head bowed, punishing her hair with a large, gilt backed hairbrush.

'Ninety eight, ninety nine, a hundred,' Angela lifted her head and flicked back her hair with a practiced gesture. Her face was flushed from bending down, her legs apart, her body braced stiffly as her mother had taught her, putting her full weight into dragging the brush through her unruly hair. She breathed heavily from the effort.

Jack, leaning against the door looking at her reflection in the mirror, idly rubbing his own hair with a towel, said, 'you know, don't you, that that's a complete waste of time. Just an old wives' tale.'

'It stimulates the scalp,' she replied automatically, the standard response to the standard criticism.

'You never look at things logically,' he sighed. 'It doesn't make sense that brushing your hair a hundred times does any more than get rid of tangles.' He observed himself in the dressing table mirror. His own hair was beginning to thin, the masculine M shape of his hairline getting more pronounced. He roughly chafed his head with the towel. 'Why not two hundred, or fifty, or ninety two?' he asked, and murmured, staring into his own eyes, 'no sense whatsoever.'

Angela sighed, 'Well, darling,' she said, putting the hairbrush down and smiling up at his reflection, 'I'm sure you're right. Just a silly idea my mother had.'

Jack stood behind her and placed a hand on each of her shoulders. His eyes held hers in the mirror before he leaned to kiss her on the shoulder. 'That's my girl,' he whispered in her ear. As he turned to go back into the bathroom to hang his towel carefully on the drying rail, he said, 'Oh, by the way, isn't it your day for the shrink?'

'Yes,' she said, 'Tuesday for the therapist.'

'Sounds like another waste of time to me,' Jack threw over his shoulder.

'I really think it's doing me good, Jack. Don't you think I'm more relaxed, more my old self.'

'Can't see any difference frankly,' replied her husband, 'you still look like a rabbit caught in the headlights to me. God knows how you ever got through life, when everything sends you into a tizz.'

'I don't know why you married me, Jack.'

'Because I love you, silly. Once you get back on your feet we can think about that baby you're always going on about, although frankly the timing couldn't be worse with the Singapore merger coming up next month.'

Instead of answering him, she said, casually, 'Dr Fisher was asking about you.'

'Oh?' said Jack, absently, and then, 'Oh, no you don't my girl. You're not dragging me off to your guru.'

'He does think it would be helpful if we both spoke to him.' Angela turned and leaned towards her husband, looking up into his face. 'Please Jack. I really need you there.'

'And I need to get my wife back,' Jack said loudly. 'The girl who sang while she worked. The girl who's laughter I could hear in my dreams. The girl who couldn't wait to see me, who threw her arms around me and didn't care what anyone thought. Where has that girl gone, Angela? Who is this quiet, nervous person who creeps around the house, and has panic attacks and has to give up her job because she's always in such a state? Who are you?' he pointed at her reflection. Where has that Angela gone?' He was shouting now, pacing across the bedroom, swinging the towel in one hand, waving wildly in the air with the other.

'I don't know,' she whispered, 'I just don't know.'

Jack flung open the door of the dressing room. 'Look at the mess in here,' he shouted, his voice muffled as he stepped inside to choose a shirt. Suits were lined up, facing towards the window, saluting the morning, in the left hand side of the wardrobe; next to them were a dozen shirts, all facing the same way as the suits, three blue, three white, three striped and three in a soft tan, followed by sports gear, golf, tennis, rugby. The other side of the room was taken up with Angela's clothes and shoes, muted shades of beige, lilac, cream and caramel. 'When did you last iron a shirt for me? Look at all this clutter in here. Where the hell is my squash gear? You know I always play today.'

When she made no response, he turned towards her, rubbed vigorously at the space between his eyebrows, and sighed.

'Oh, Angela,' he said, crossing the room and sitting beside her on the bed. 'You mustn't mind me. I'm always shooting my mouth off. My shirts are fine. I just want you to be well again.' He made to take her in his arms, but stopped himself and reached for her hand and held it in his. Angela looked up into his face, her eyes blank.

'What's happening to me, Jack?' she whispered, 'everything used to be so lovely.'

'And it will be again,' he cried with force, his eyes bright. He touched her hand to his forehead. 'Just as soon as you're well.'

A car horn tooted outside, and Jack looked up, startled. 'I must go,' he said, 'you rest. We'll go out for dinner somewhere lovely tonight. I have to go,' he repeated, 'the car's here. I'll ring you at lunchtime.' He took his jacket from the back of the chair and rushed out of the room.

She got up slowly and walked into the dressing room and stood for some minutes considering the racks of her clothing. She walked dreamily along the row of garments, touching some, taking some off the rail to examine more closely. From an upper shelf she pulled down a large oval box covered in a snowdrop and leaf design with a lid to match. She put the box on a low chair, lifted the lid and with an uncharacteristic flourish withdrew a red dress. The sight was so shocking to her that she looked around furtively, but then nodded and smiled to herself. She draped the dress over the velvety back of the chair and closed the door, gliding silently across the floor towards the bathroom.

Angela arrived five minutes early for her appointment and sat rigidly on a chair in the waiting room. The red dress dramatised the pallor of her face. She crossed her ankles and spread the skirt modestly around her legs.. Her shoes were black, with a fashionably high heel. She clutched a large black purse. Her hair was drawn back into a loose chignon, tied with a black chiffon scarf, and escaping wisps of hair brushed her face and neck. She smiled coolly at the receptionist and lowered her head into a back issue of Vogue. At exactly two o'clock Dr Fisher's office door opened and he stepped into the waiting room.

'Mrs Cassidy,' he smiled at her, 'on time as always,' and ushered her into his room.

When she had arranged herself carefully on the chair in front of his desk, Angela watched Paul Fisher as he polished his glasses, briefly flicked though some notes in a green folder, and, without asking her, poured two cups of coffee from a small espresso machine near the window, added cream to one and stirred it thoughtfully. Then he approached her, handed her the coffee with the cream and, ignoring his own cup, sat on the edge of the desk, leaning forward towards her. She raised her eyes to his, and then quickly looked down at the cup in her hands.

'Angela,' he said simply.

'I asked him to come,' she said quickly, and gave a small, self-conscious laugh.

'And he said no,' offered Dr Fisher. She nodded, gripping the cup and saucer, still not able to raise her eyes.

'Well then,' he said, 'it's just the two of us.' He leaned forward to ease a stray wisp of hair behind her ear.

WEATHER FORECAST

HE ARRIVED SOON after the lunch break, bracing himself for the exchange ahead. Last night's fight had left them both exhausted. Coming home early was a concession to her, a choreographed gesture to show that he was anxious to repair the damage. He left his site manager, Eddie, in charge, 'I'm taking an early mark, Ed.' He crouched down under a cold tap to wash cement dust from his eyes. When he got to his house his hair was still wet, bristling in the harsh light.

On the front lawn, in random piles, were shoes and boots; most of his clothes; hundreds of compact discs; tools, a rusty barbecue plate dragged out of the shed and his fishing gear. The garage door was closed and all the blinds in the house down; the façade stared blankly at him. Her car was parked in the driveway, backed up tight to the garage.

He squinted into the sunlight. The trousers of his dinner suit had been roughly hacked about knee length, the two amputated limbs flung haphazardly and clutched in the arms of a scarlet bougainvillea. He backed up and drove away the way he had come.

Turning onto the coast road he stopped at a clearing, facing the horizon. He dragged his fingers through his damp hair and leaned his forehead briefly on the still burning steering wheel, then looked hard for a while at the crystal sky, drumming his fingers on the steering wheel to the rhythmic roar of the surf crashing on the rocks below.

When he got to the yard, Eddie was unloading. 'I'm taking the truck, Eddie, the small one. Dunno how long for.'

'Righto,' said Eddie, 'I filled her up this morning.'

'That's OK,' he replied, 'I won't be going far.' He parked his car by the shed where it would get the afternoon shade, and lashed some supplies onto the one-ton truck. When he got back to his house again, the truck was sitting low from the weight of the load.

He glanced at the house; the blinds were still drawn, and the car still in the driveway. He paced out the front lawn; found an area sufficiently level, under the patchy shelter of a jacaranda tree. Here he erected a two-room tent, bright red with a striped awning. He angled it side on so that the opening was hidden from the road and the house. Under the awning he set up a gas barbecue, a hanging lantern, and a large cooler box. He positioned a director's chair and a folding card table in the meagre shade, took a can of beer from the cooler box, and smiled at the soft hiss it made when he dragged on the ring pull. He raised his beer in salute to the house and then sprawled in the chair, talking quietly into his mobile phone.

The sun was dropping fast so he lit a ring of mosquito coils around the tent. The cold beer went down his throat in a hurry, and he crushed the can in his hand and threw it onto the driveway in front of the parked car. Half way through his second beer, which he took more slowly, a pizza van drew up and he paid the delivery boy and settled down to eat. Just before the dusk that fell like a blow in the sub tropics, another truck pulled up and two men delivered a portable toilet, intense blue with 'Portaloo' printed in large yellow script on three sides. This he located on the driveway, with the entrance facing the house, blocking the car.

When dark fell, the lights went on in the house and he could hear the dull hum of the air conditioner and see the blue flickering light the television cast across what used to be the kids' rumpus room. The phone in the hallway rang regularly throughout the evening, although voices were too low to hear. When he'd eaten and sent the pizza box the way of the beer cans, he turned his portable player up loud and let Bruce Springstein compete with the clatter of the cicadas.

One of his neighbours passed by, walking the dog. 'Nice night for a barbecue,' she called to him.

'Couldn't be better,' he replied. He waved his beer can at her and she carried on down the road, dragged at arm's length by a witless bishon frise. 'Nosey cow,' he mouthed at her back.

At eleven o'clock, he dowsed the lamp and turned off the music. The lights in the house were now out except for the glare of the kitchen light spilling over the back verandah. The suburban street was suddenly still.

Next morning the sun appeared as abruptly as it had gone, and battered his eyelids through the flimsy canvas of the tent. He rose and set a kettle to boil, humming softly as he raided the cooler box for chunks of bread and cheese. The sky blared relentless blue. Just after nine a taxi pulled up and hooted its horn. The front door of the house flew open, and his wife rushed down the steps.

'What the hell do you think you're doing?' she asked him.

'Going out?' he said.

'I'm going to see my solicitor,' she hissed and sped off in the taxi.

He gathered some of the clothes from around the garden and neatly spread t-shirts and jeans along the railing of the front verandah. He pulled an extending ladder from the truck, and laced several pairs of work boots along the horizontal bar of the television aerial where they glistened in the glare - paint and cement splattered bunting. Tony, from next door strolled over and surveyed the scene for a few moments from the verge of the grass, saying nothing.

'G'day Tone, great weather again. Forecast says rain. Haven't seen much signs of it yet.'

Tony cleared his throat. 'Having a spot of bother on the home front, I see. Don't worry, pal, she'll soon come round. They always do.' They were both silent after that, until Tony cleared his throat again and shuffled off.

The following morning the taxi appeared again, and as his wife rushed past him, head lowered, he called out to her, insistently cheerful, 'Hope you've got your brolly. There's rain forecast.' She ignored him as she picked her way through the pile of debris growing on the driveway.

He unloaded a wheelbarrow, a sack of sand and one of cement, and carefully prepared the mix after digging a large hole near the house. A twelve foot length of four by four went into the hole after he had secured a bar across the top. He levelled the whole thingoff and cemented the post well in. In this weather it would set quickly. From the t-bar he had strung a length of strong rope looped about seven feet off the ground.

An old Toyota pulled up, and a young, blonde, surfer stuck his head out the window. 'You having a garage sale mate?' he called.

'No. No I'm not. I'm not having a garage sale.'

'Oh, ok. I just thought...with all the stuff and that...'

'No.'

When his wife came home, what was left of his dinner suit was on a hanger, fully dressed with a white frilled shirt and black bow tie and swinging from the looped rope of the pole.

The following afternoon Eddie screeched up, flinging himself out of the van, waving a large envelope.

'Look,' he shouted before he was fully out of the van, 'we got the contract for the Marina. Bloody ripper, mate. There's two years work here. Gotta get moving.' For the first time he glanced around. 'What's the story here, then?' he said.

'No story. I'm just having a quiet Foster's. Care to join me? It's icy cold.'

'Jesus, Tom, what the hell's going on? When are you coming back to work? If we don't start on this Marina job straight away we'll lose the contract.'

'I'm a bit busy right now Ed.'

'Doing what? Drinking beer in the front yard? What's that bloody great gallows doing there? I thought public hangings went out centuries ago.'

He held his hands out wide in a helpless gesture. 'I'm just drying my clothes, Ed, before it rains.'

'Rain?' said Eddie, his hat pulled low over his eyes to deflect the glare, 'what rain? There isn't a cloud between here and Alice Springs.'

'Oh,' said Tom, ' there's a storm brewing right enough.'

Going Home

Straining, she could hear the familiar jangle of a horse's harness. That must be the milk delivery. If the milkman found her, he would tell the housekeeper where she was, and she would be dragged back to the house and into that dark, dirty scullery. Mrs Piper beat her when she was slow, and she never had enough to eat. Jack, the stable boy used to wink at her when he came in for his breakfast, but nobody else spoke to her at all. She missed her sisters. Young Mr Wallsingham stared at her if she met him in the hallway, and one day barred her way, and said he would not let her pass until she gave him a kiss. When Mrs Piper came out of the drawing room with a tea tray, he stepped back and made a low, mocking bow to let her pass.

Each evening she trudged the back stairs to her attic, and washed with cold water and an old rag, but sometimes she just fell into bed, exhausted. Last night long after she had put out her candle she heard young Mr Wallsingham, on the landing, calling her name in a hoarse whisper. She cowered silently behind the door and finally he skulked down the stairs as quietly as he had come. When the sounds of the house stilled, she dressed fully and crept out by the kitchen door. It would be light soon. She would hide until night, and then make her way home. She crept in to the coal cellar and huddled in the corner.

She heard the scrape of the latch on the trapdoor.

'Five hundredweight today is it, Mrs Piper?' a man's voice called, and she shrank from the light as the hatch was dragged back, and the first nuggets fell.

EYRIE

'THOSE INTERFERING do gooders should have left well enough alone. We haven't had a golden eagle in this country for nearly one hundred years, and I'm telling you they weren't missed. So what do they do? Bring the rotten things back, that's what. Import them from Scotland, no less, and put little satellites on them in case, the lord save us, they should lose any of the little darlings. Well, they won't get the better of me, I can tell you. I have a right and a responsibility to defend my property.'

'Grandpa, the golden eagle is a protected species.'

'Not from me they're not. Pass me my boots.'

'But Grandpa, they have as much right to be here as we do.'

'Well, you and I don't go round killing sheep.'

'What? What the hell else do we do with them.'

'Don't get smart with me young fellow, you know full well what I mean. These eagles will take sheep that belong to me, that I need to sell to keep this family fed and housed. Aren't you the one that showed me the film of that eagle taking a goat.'

'But they were bigger eagles in America,' wailed Danny.

'I don't care where it was. You look at that and tell me I shouldn't be worried.' Joe jumped up from tying his boots. 'If they can take goats in America, they can take sheep in Donegal, and they're not having mine.'

'They live on small animals that live near to the ground, rabbits and hares and mice.'

Joe stomped down to the hallway, and started to haul wet weather gear from the cupboard under the stairs. Danny hovered behind him, talking all the while, 'those birds are native to this area, they're beautiful and majestic.'

'They're murdering great raptors and scavengers, and you can't make me see them as cuddly little chicks.'

'You could get prosecuted,' tried Danny, as a last resort, while his grandfather selected a stout stick for the rough upland blanket bog of Glenveagh National Park. 'You're planning to enter a national park, find an eagle's nest, most probably on a cliff face, and destroy the eggs. And the rangers will stay in the visitors' centre drinking cups of tea, I suppose. What will you do then, old man, a sweep of the counties, maybe? They've been recorded in Derry, Fermanagh, Sligo, Kerry even?'

'Mocking me won't make any difference. They say these birds have been persecuted. It's the farmers of Donegal who are being persecuted by these thieving devils.'

Danny walked up and down the kitchen, dragging his hand through his hair, watching his grandfather make tea and pour it into a flask, pack cheese and chocolate and apples into an old army knapsack.

'How long do you expect to be out there?' said Danny. 'As long as it takes,' said his grandfather, without lifting his head. 'Early in the morning is my best chance.'

Danny snorted in disgust. 'So you're going to camp out in the bog for the night and kill chicks before breakfast? Is that a sensible thing for a man of your age to be doing?'

Joe turned then and looked straight at his grandson, his voice softer now. 'Look son,' he said, 'my family have run sheep on these god forsaken hills for generations. It's a hard enough way for a man to make a living, without a crowd of bleeding hearts bringing back birds of prey that we were damn glad to see the back of.'

Bag packed, Joe went out to the shed, looking for weed killer. Danny knew well what could be used for poison, paraquat or the stuff they had to treat liver fluke in the sheep. He watched as the old man foraged in the freezer looking for pieces of meat to put the poison into as bait.

'Anyway,' Joe said over his shoulder, 'I'm not fool enough to go climbing up the cliff face to find chicks. I'd probably be attacked myself. Do you know how big those eagles get? And the females bigger than the males. No, I'll just find a nice isolated place in the heather and leave the baits. They can come and collect their own dinner, it's not room service I'm providing.' He smiled at Danny, trying to include him in the little joke but Danny refused to look at him, and kept his gaze firmly on the snow clouds he could see forming out the small window.

'The forecast is for snow,' he said loudly.

'They'll be good and hungry then,' said Joe

'You'll catch your death out there,' said Danny, 'is there any way I can talk you out of such foolishness.'

'Let me be,' said Joe, and took matches and a piece of rope out of the drawer. He crammed an old blanket into his knapsack and put on his favourite cap. 'I'm ready now. Stop worrying. I'm only looking out for what's mine. It's what any man would do,' and the door slammed and he was gone. Danny shook his head and went into the hallway to pull on his boots.

Joe did not really intend to spend the night, but felt driven to say it. Wait till he had a family of his own, he thought, he'll see things differently then. His plan now was to walk some ways into the park away from the tourists and leave his baits and get out before the park closed. He knew full well how dangerous it could be in the bog land; a man could disappear in among the heather and never be found. Perhaps, he smiled grimly to himself, they should be putting a little satellite around my leg. He put the meat for bait into a smaller bag so that he could look as if he was just another tourist out for the day. He put the blanket in the boot, and then changed his mind, and crammed it in the bag with the bait.

He knew also that this would be the best time of year to see Golden Eagles in the park, as the winter days were still short. The birds should be clearly visible to the naked eye if he watched carefully enough. He had been coming to the park for more than twenty years and knew his way around, and where to go to have the best chance of sighting at least one of the raptors as it hunted. He wanted to stay on the lowland where there was plenty of cover from oak and hazel. Higher up, the summits and crags where the eagles built their eyries, were much more sparsely covered with vegetation and shrubs. He did not want to risk being seen setting the bait, and for all his bravado, he had no confidence that he had the strength any more to make the climb, and he could see the snow on the peaks. No, he said to himself, I'll set my bait and get at least one of the devils that way.

He left the path and set off into the trees. The bedrock in the bog was deeply fissured, and he needed to take great care crossing the gullies and joints in the rock. He pushed through bell heather where it was drier and then deer grass and bog cotton where the moisture built up in the ground. There was no sign of deer or meadow pipits; it was too early in the year to see any but the boldest wildlife.

He didn't have far to go now, and began to feel uneasy. He seemed to be feeling the cold more than he ever used to, as he followed his laboured breath deeper into the bog. He began to regret the flask of tea left in the car; it would have warmed him.

He was startled by a sudden rustling on his left, and stood still, trying to locate the sound. As he made to move on he heard it again, and cocked his head to one side, taking off his cap to make a horn to put to his ear. There was no sound, so he put his cap back on and started off again, and the rustling came again. He turned, then, and set off towards the sound, and trod slowly and carefully, listening all the time. Again he heard the rustling close by. As he rounded the hillside he saw, face down in the heather, a large eagle, wings outstretched. It was a dark brown bird with a smooth golden sheen coming on its head, but there were still some white feathers on the tail, so it was a very young bird, and he could see where it was tagged. Some of the feathers on one of its wings looked to be broken or bent, and the sound Joe had heard was the bird thrashing its wings, trying to lift itself off the ground. He stood completely still, watching, as it attempted to take off. He moved around to the side, and when the bird could see him it made just a small attempt to rear up. It was getting weaker. The old man looked around at the hills and the sky, and then examined the bird again. It was as fine a specimen as you could wish. A predator of that size and strength would have no natural enemy. Except me, perhaps, thought Joe, isn't this what I wanted, to kill eagles? To save my flock?

He put his bag carefully on the ground and pulled out the old blanket and the rope. He circled the bird very slowly, and when he was behind it he rushed forward and threw the blanket over its head. The bird began to thrash again and let out a high ke ke sound, but suddenly drew its wings closer to its body and Joe managed to hold it down with the blanket and secure it with the rope.

He staggered, exhausted, as the night was drawing in, back to the visitors' centre and called for a ranger to take the bird from him. When the eagle was taken inside for treatment, Joe fell heavily onto a seat, and bent over, trying to catch his breath. When he lifted his head, Danny was standing in front of him. 'So, granddad,' he said, 'I see you struck a blow for the sheep farmer.'

'I don't know what you're laughing at,' Joe gasped, 'It's about time, young fellow, you learned that these birds have just as much right to be here as we do.

Moving House

'THAT BLASTED CAT gets better fed than I do,' roared Arthur from the kitchen, scowling at his makeshift lunch. 'I get a cheese sandwich and he gets roast beef.'

'Never you mind, my precious,' she whispered into the soft fur of her beloved Sultan. 'We don't care about grouchy old Arthur do we? Taking us out of our lovely home to go and live in some horrible holiday shack on the beach. I don't like the beach, and you won't either will you, my dear little pet. This is so upsetting, all this packing up. You mustn't be frightened. I'll look after you.'

Arthur stomped into the living room with an old fishing basket. 'This will do to take that spoiled animal on the trip. I'm not throwing good money after bad buying a special cage for his majesty. Come to think of it, this clasp looks a bit loose. Maybe we'll lose the little beggar on the way, eh?' He leered into Marjorie's face, and with a jolt of fear she reached to examine the basket.

'Just joking,' he said. 'For God's sake, has that cat got you so befuddled you can't take a joke anymore?' He shuffled off, grumbling, to line the basket with newspaper for the journey. Sultan sprang from the couch just in time to cross Arthur's path, making him stumble against the door and he cursed loudly.

Ever since Marjorie had bought her beautiful chinchilla cat three years ago, Sultan had caused arguments. Arthur thought she cared for the cat more than she cared for him, and she thought that Arthur's jealousy bordered on paranoia, and they were both right. Sultan's serene presence focussed their attention on all the grudges and hurts that had been festering in their marriage for years.

'The catalyst,' her sister would say, enjoying the pun.

Their life of quietly shared bitterness, over Arthur's lack of promotions and Marjorie's inability to have children, had become the refrain that accompanied their every exchange. Neither of them seemed able or even willing to break through the barricade of animosity they had so solidly built up through disappointments piled on failures. They survived their barren marriage nursing an array of old hurts and resentments. Arthur had never been successful enough in the police force in his wife's opinion. It shamed her that he was still going to work in a sergeant's uniform until retirement, when all the recruits who started with him had climbed up the promotional ladder and left him far behind. His father had risen to chief inspector in the Australian Federal Police and Arthur was expected to follow in his footsteps. He was convinced that his father was jealous of him, and had somehow sabotaged his advancement from the sidelines, not wanting his son's achievements to overshadow his own. Any ambitions the young Arthur held for advancement jelled over his career into sullenness and frustration as the years passed and the promotions dried up. He accused Marjorie of not supporting him fully, and in some ways this was probably true. She had long since grown tired of his rants against his colleagues, and the parlous state of the youth of today. His rigid adherence to the most trivial point of protocol stifled creativity and shoe-horned him into a lumpen existence behind a desk, filing reports that he was sure nobody ever read.

But her greatest tragedy and Arthur's greatest bitterness was their failure to produce any children. His hope of a son and heir to take his place in the world proudly beside him was shattered, and her dream of a large family and domestic contentment morphed in a thickening fog of disenchantment as time wore away their initial joy in one another, and replaced it with petty griping and point scoring. What Arthur took to be sweetness and compliance in his young bride, he came to see as weakness and lack of spirit. Her bold hero, ready to take on the world and mould it to his satisfaction, became, in her eyes, a critical and carping old man bowed down by the petty vicissitudes of life. They had never seriously considered parting, although it had been threatened by both often enough. 'You make your bed, and you lie on it' Arthur's mother had impressed on him and Marjorie believed the same. Now that Arthur had retired he had decided to leave the house they had lived in for forty years and move to their holiday home on the beach near Bateman's Bay on the south coast of New South Wales. They had bought the small chalet many years ago and Arthur had relentlessly insisted that they spend every January there. 'What's the point of having a house by the sea, and then gallivanting off to Bali, or some such, to be fleeced by the natives and lie on their beach when we're a spit away from our own - the most beautiful beach in the most beautiful country in the world. Complete waste of money, if you ask me, traipsing around the world when you can see the whole world on those travel programs you can never keep your eyes off. You must think I'm made of money. Is there any more tea in that pot?' Marjorie sighed and put the tour brochures in the recycle bin as she went into the kitchen to make more tea.

'We can rent out this house,' he had said, 'It'll give us a bit more income.' Marjorie put a tight lid on her resentment, apart from ignored comments about being consulted about what happened to her life. She did not want to move, she loved her home and had friends and extended family within easy reach. She foresaw a bleak existence in a small village, with much more of Arthur's company than she had anticipated or relished. Having him underfoot after his retirement, criticising and offering unwanted suggestions for doing chores that she had been doing efficiently and smoothly all her life, had tried her patience. She dreaded the prospect of being in a new environment, knowing no one, and having no escape from his faultfinding presence. Her husband was keen, however, to distance himself from the scene of his disappointments and failures and foresaw a glowing future of fishing and swimming, and drinking beer in the twilight.

Arthur came back into the room and said, 'Perhaps we can teach his majesty to swim. They get quite a few sharks down that way.' This idea seemed to cheer him up for a while.

'No wonder,' said her sister, witnessing their dealings with each other one day, 'no wonder they rate moving house nearly as high on the list of stressors as losing a spouse.'

'Higher in some cases, I would think,' said Marjorie grimly, flinging Arthur's favourite corduroy trousers into the skip on the front lawn.

Finally moving day arrived. They, or rather Arthur, had decided to let the house furnished and make do with the few things that were in their holiday cottage, despite Marjorie's feeble protests. 'We've a better chance of renting it furnished, and anyway, we've got everything we need on the coast.' He said, and his wife winced at the prospect of endless sand and Formica, and makeshift bedding.

When they were finally set to make the journey, they fell, exhausted, into the car with a yowling Sultan squeezed into the fishing basket, on the back seat.

'It's alright Sultan,' Marjorie cooed in an attempt to calm her precious pet. 'It's only a little car journey,' she lied, 'we'll soon be at our lovely new house.'

'I told you to get a sedative from the vet,' said Arthur. 'Can't you see, woman, that when you keep prattling on to him, it only makes him worse? For pity's sake keep him quiet or I'll put him in the boot.' Marjorie subsided into silent worry, but Sultan, unaware of all but his discomfort and fear, continued to scratch and complain. 'At least I would if there was room,' said Arthur to his horrified wife. 'I won't be able to put up with that caterwauling all the way.'

As they left Canberra and the only life either of them had ever known, the house empty as the agent had not yet been able to find suitable tenants, Marjorie slumped into her seat and refused even to look back. Her eyes filled with tears she dare not shed for fear of more of Arthur's criticism, so she sniffed discreetly to the chorus of her cat's mewing.

After an hour, Arthur declared that he was due to stretch his legs and have a break from driving. 'That's what they say isn't it?' he cried, ' 'Rest, revive, survive, '' he quoted the advertisement on the billboards. They pulled into a garage with ample room for him to walk around and do some stretching exercises. Marjorie and Sultan sat in mutual misery in the car, parked in the open with the sun blinding their eyes. When Arthur had finished his callisthenics, he sat back into the car and drummed on the steering wheel, humming to himself. 'What a day.' He said, ' couldn't be better. Absolutely perfect. New life, marvellous.' He turned on the ignition and then turned it off again. 'Why don't you get us a coffee?' he said to his wife, 'I need to keep alert for the drive.'

'I could take over for a while,' she said, knowing what the answer would be.

'No, no, I'll do it,' he said, ' just get the coffee and we'll be on our way. Try and keep that bloody cat quiet. Can't stand women drivers anyway.' He mumbled, as if she couldn't hear him.

Marjorie climbed out of the car and walked slowly into the shop, bought coffee for Arthur and headed back to the car. She handed him the cup and he took a sip.

'For God's sake, woman, there's no sugar in it. Can't you do a simple thing like get a cup of coffee without getting it wrong? Forty years I've been putting up with your stupidity and you still can't get a simple thing like a cup of coffee right.'

'Oh, said Marjorie, flustered. 'I'll go and get some.'

'Don't bother. I'll get it myself. At least that way I'll get it done properly.'

She sat in the car watching his indignant back as he stormed into the shop. Sultan went suddenly quiet, and she savoured the silence. She looked into the basket on the rear seat to make sure he was comfortable, opened the car door and walked around the car. As she sat into the driver's seat, a small smile touched her pale lips.

‘Won’t be long now, darling,’ she said to the cat. She turned on the ignition, put the indicator on, and slowly drove the car away in the direction they had come.

Shopkeeping

Wednesday was ice day. After school his stepmother sent him, with a sack and the exact money, to get ice. The shop had an old ice chest and a large block of ice was put in the bottom cavity once a week when cream and butter were delivered. With luck the ice would last for three days in the summer and nearly a week in the winter. The ice box was kept in the store room, with a small hose leading out through a hole his father had drilled in the outside wall to let the water run into the yard as the ice melted. There was always a dank, filmy puddle to be crossed in the narrow alleyway outside the storeroom door. Peter's job was to take the sack up the high street and buy a large block of ice and carry it back at a run. As he ran, with the sack slung over his shoulder, the ice banged against his back, and cold water and dripped onto the back of his legs and into his socks.

Just beside the puddle in the passageway, on the broken concrete sat a rusty Oxo tin. The egg man, who delivered once a week, would only replace a bad or broken egg if he saw the evidence. Into the Oxo tin went bad eggs and Peter was sent to fetch the tin, and open it for the rotten eggs to be inspected and counted. Then he dug a hole in the tiny square of earth in the yard and buried the contents. In the summer the contents of the tin would squirm with maggots, and Peter knew to hold his breath as he opened it up.

At closing time it was Peter's job to put the unsold vegetables in the storeroom where it was cooler than the shop, and to sweep out and wash the floor after turning the 'Open' sign around and locking the door. Hardly a night went by without someone banging on the door and making apologetic faces at him through the glass, wanting him to let them in for something they had forgotten. He would have liked to ignore them, but, as his father said, 'business is business' so he would open the door and serve them and try not to mind when they tramped all over the wet floor leaving dirty footprints that he had to mop over again. One particular night he washed the bit of floor inside the door five times before he finally got to put out the light and go to the kitchen for his supper.

Friday was 'tick' day. His stepmother gave credit to a few customers, and when they failed to pay up on payday, Peter was sent to their houses to collect. In his school satchel he carried an exercise book which recorded their names and addresses, what they had bought, the date and the amount owing. Friday evening, just after the men at the factory had been paid, Peter would tap quietly on the various doors. When someone answered he just stood there holding the book in one hand and a cloth bank bag in the other and never spoke. Everyone knew who he was and why he was there.

Last week one of the big sons answered the door at the first house, and with a toss of the head called out down the darkened hallway, 'It's the kid from the shop, Mum.' Then he heard a muffled fumbling in what sounded like the tea caddy at home, and another son, David, who was in Peter's class at school and a good head taller than him, was sent to the door to pay him some money, 'And you be sure you watch him mark it off,' he heard the mother shout. David sauntered down the hall, scuffing his feet on the worn lino, and dropped a half a crown at Peter's feet. 'You want it, you get it,' he snarled. As Peter leaned down to pick up the coin, David feinted a punch at his head, hopped back and forth, taking up a boxing stance. 'Put it in the book, you snivelling little git,' he said. Peter fumbled for the right page and subtracted two shillings and sixpence from the total. 'Now get lost, before I knock your stupid shop keeping head off,' he said, as he banged his fists together as if they were gloved.

At the next house a small girl answered the door, and ran down the hall yelling for her mother. He could hear the husband say, 'you'd better give him the gas money. She's got no right sending that poor kid to do her dirty work.' At the third house the mother came to the door herself, and quickly pushed the door half shut, so that her husband couldn't see who was on the doorstep. She scrabbled in her apron pocket for a bit of change to give him, to get rid of him, but there was no money there. 'Tell your mum,' she whispered hoarsely, 'I'll be down Monday morning, definite, to pay off what I owe.' Peter was on strict instructions not to leave a house until he got paid something, so he shuffled from one foot to the other, not sure what to do next. They both jumped when a man's voice called out from the rear of the house, 'Who's at the door then, Lil?' 'Just someone looking for number 4,' Lil called back. 'What's the matter with em? Can't they read?' came the husband's voice before being overcome by coughing. Lil looked at Peter with pleading, watery eyes, and he nodded and moved away, pausing only to write 'Coming in Monday' in the book. At the next house, the curtain twitched but no sound came from inside and nobody answered the door. He half-heartedly knocked again, and then wrote 'Out' carefully in the book. Of his six calls he got no answer at three houses and his relief was dampened by the knowledge that he would be accused of not going to the houses at all. All he went home with was one half crown and the shilling gas money.

His stepmother had told him he was old enough to learn that life was not all beer and skittles, and it was about time he started pulling his weight with the shop. 'You needn't think you're going to be treated like a guest in this house,' she said. 'We all have to do jobs we don't like in this world, so stop complaining and get out there. The sooner you get back the sooner you can have your supper.'

One Friday as he emerged from the front door of the shop, Mrs Brown, who usually detoured to the shop in the next street, was passing by. She had her daughter with her, a large short sighted girl with NHS glasses and lank, greasy hair. The two of them were trying to rush past the shop with their heads down, hoping not to be spotted. Mrs Brown had owed money for weeks, ever since her husband had been put off from the factory. 'See what happens?' said his stepmother, 'You not only lose the money they owe you, but you lose the customer as well, cause they can't look you in the face and have to go and get tick from some other poor fool who'll give it to them.' They were nearly past the shop when the daughter, her chin so low on her chest she could hardly see where she was going, stumbled into a box of potatoes that were propped outside the shop with a 'Special' sticker on them. The box went over with a clatter and there were potatoes rolling across the pavement in all directions and into the gutter. Peter took chase and picked some of them up. Mrs Brown dragged on her daughter's sleeve to make her keep moving but the child stood stock still and wailed at the top of her voice. Peter's stepmother heard the commotion and hurried out, 'Ah, Mrs Brown, I've been hoping to catch you.' She cried. Peter dropped the potatoes he had gathered back into the box, wiped his hands on his trousers, and headed off down the road to his first house.

He wanted to ask his father to be let off the job of collecting money. 'Dad,' he said one morning, finding his father alone in the kitchen. He had his back to Peter and was standing with one foot on a wooden chair, polishing his shoes. He was dressed for work, and had his small cardboard suitcase sitting on the floor near his chair. That meant he would be away for days at his job as a travelling salesman. 'What is it, son?' he said without looking up, brushing his shoe as if it had offended him. Peter ran his finger along the top of the chair back, and cleared his throat. Just then he heard his stepmother's tread on the stairs. 'What?' said his father, looking up at him. 'Oh, nothing,' said Peter moving out of the line of the door as she came in. 'Good.' said his father, 'Couldn't be less, could it? I've got to get going. Mind you behave now while I'm away, and do what you're told.' He grabbed his suitcase, kissed his wife briefly and rushed out to his car. Peter watched him drive away, and tried to wave, although boxes obscured the rear window of the car, and his father would not have been able see him standing on the step in his socks, waving.

When his father was home, the three of them sat in silence eating breakfast at the kitchen table. When his father was not at home, it was his morning job to put the vegetables out on display and, just as he left for school, open the shop door and call up the stairs that he was going. His stepmother was out of bed and dressed by then, and they usually managed to avoid meeting. This was Peter's favourite time. He had long since perfected the art of pushing a few sweets into his pockets, or a handful of broken biscuits although the crumbs threatened to give him away. The till was just a drawer under the counter and he discovered that if he opened it just a little, he could reach his hand in and stop the little bell at the back from tinkling. Once a week or so he risked this dangerous manoeuvre and pocketed a three penny bit or sixpence, his heart pounding in his ears. If he set the bell off, his stepmother would hear it and wonder why she could not hear the voice of a customer. Since she moved quickly and quietly there was a real danger that she would appear behind him and catch him, literally, with his hand in the till. The chance of being discovered and punished made his victory all the sweeter. His favourite thing was a Wagon Wheel, but he could only manage one of these when the shelf was overcrowded and a single one would not be missed.

After Tuesday's science class he kicked a football around the schoolyard with his mates and missed his usual bus. He ran all the way home, and arrived just before closing, emptying crumbs out of his pockets as he went.

'Where the hell have you been? No, don't bother with any of your lies, just get that box put out the back.'

He rushed to pick up a box of carrots to take to the storeroom. A few of them slid off the top of the crate. As he bent to pick them up, he remembered Mrs Brown's daughter and the potatoes disappearing down the drain, and bit back a small smile.

Cousin From America

Now, where would you like to go today? I know how important it is to make plans on your holiday or the days drift by and you haven't seen anything of the country. Of course your parents would have told you a lot about Ireland, God rest their souls, but the place has changed immensely since they left. Times were bad in the 50's when so many young people had to go to England and America and Australia just to find work. There was nothing here, I'm afraid. If I hadn't followed my own father into the drapery business I expect I would have ended up one of those poor benighted souls, hanging over the railings of the ship to catch a last glimpse of their homeland, shivering in insufficient clothing, patched and worn as it was, and passed down from son to son. But, now, you don't want to hear my sad tales. I suppose you'll want to see where your grandfather's house was, not there anymore, I'm afraid, just a few bits of ruins, and the school he tramped across the fields to, all that's left of that is one of the front pillars of the gate that you can see the name, 'Walstown School', still faintly on there.

Mallow is a lot like an Irish conversation I always think, you can never get anywhere directly. You spend your whole time going round corners and round roundabouts and through traffic lights, instead of going in a straight line to where you want to be. God knows, you could spend the whole day in this town going around, like a spinning top. You'd be too young to remember the spinning tops. When I was a boy we had no toys to speak of and we'd make our own. I often whittled a spinning top, for my sisters mostly, because the boys preferred ball games as a general rule. We made our own fun, not like the youngsters of today who want everything laid on, and expensive things too – computer games and hand held games, and they wouldn't bring in a stick of wood for the fire. And they're always bored, we were never bored, we didn't have time to be bored, and by God, if you had nothing to do, your parents would soon find jobs for you to be doing. 'The devil makes work for idle hands,' my father used to say, and if he caught you looking the least bit faraway or not busy, he'd soon be putting a saw or a hammer or a milk pail in your hand. If you didn't want to be working all day, you quick smart found something to do with yourself. Even homework, sometimes, was preferable to the jobs that could be found for you. The young ones nowadays don't know how well off they are, and, of course, they're never satisfied. Everything they see on the television they want, and no notion of lifting a finger towards getting it. I suppose they're the same over.

Now, personally I prefer the direct approach. In America they would be used to the direct approach wouldn't they? I can't see the Americans putting up with the circumlocution that goes on here, circling round the subject until a person is dizzy. No, tell me straight, I always say, and ask me a straight question and I'll answer you to the best of my ability, get to the point as quickly as is reasonable and I won't make you wait all day for it either.

The traffic is a terror, and now they've put lights on the turn into Fair Street, we'll have to go round the other way to avoid them. Heaven knows what they want lights there for. I've been turning right and left into Fair Street for the past forty years and I never needed a traffic light yet. They're mad for telling us what to do, that's all it is, power mad politicians. And you wouldn't believe but aren't they digging up the Spa road for the umpteenth time by the way fixing the flooding. And every time there's two drops of water, the road is awash. Any sensible man could see that digging a big hole in the middle of the road won't make the rain go away any quicker. You'd have the top engineers in America wouldn't you? I think half of them are just chancers around here. Throw it up and hope for the best, or dig it down I should say, what? Ha, ha. It's good to have a bit of a laugh now and then I always say, you can't be always looking on the gloomy side. Mind you, the Irish always had a good name for making the best of things and seeing the bright side of things. But that was in the old days before the country went mad for money, and they'd trample over the top of you to get at it. Nobody has any time for anyone any more. It's dog eat dog, not like in my time where people cared about their neighbours. You could be living now in a street and neither know nor see your neighbours from one end of the year to the other. The community is gone, it's all fast cars and satellite television and blackberries they want now, and they up to their ears in debt. Is it like that over? I suppose it is. I hear the Americans are very fat, not that I'm saying you are, oh no, you're a fine figure of a man, remind me of your uncle Paddy when he was alive. Of course, the same thing's happening here. If it's good enough for the Yanks, it's good enough for us. I hope you're not offended, I mean no offence, Yanks is just a way of talking. I'm sure America is a very fine country, with fine people in it.

But never mind all that. Where would you like to go on our first morning jaunt? Not too far, I'd guess, with the rain in those black clouds just waiting for us to venture out. Mary and myself usually go shopping on a Thursday, but since she stayed home today, I hope you won't mind if we call in at the supermarket for a few bits and the paper. We like to get the paper every day to keep up with the news, not that any of it's any good, but what can you do. Of course, one time the paper would be delivered *and* the milk. These days you'd be lucky to get the letters delivered, if anyone wrote letters any more. We have a daughter in Melbourne and she either phones her mother here, or emails to our other daughter. Sure nobody writes a letter any more. Do you find that too? You'd be all on broadband over. It's all too much for me, all this dot.com business. What the hell does it mean? It's dot.com this and dot.com that. I don't understand any of it.

Oh, here's the map, if you want to check the route, or rout, as you Americans like to say. We'll head off towards Mitchelstown, see there, just above Mallow on the map, and that way we can call in and see where the old house was. There's Dan now coming in the gate. I wonder what he wants. He's my oldest neighbour and I have to tell you he's a terrible man for borrowing tools and not giving them back until you have to ask for them. Oh, that's alright, it's not me he wants he's taking Mary some eggs.

Are you comfortable enough there? The seat belt is just behind your left shoulder, and it goes in just here, can you reach? And there's a little lever to push the seat back if it's too far forward. Give yourself plenty of legroom. There's nothing worse than being cramped up with your knees up to your chin. I hear that's what it's like on those trans Atlantic flights with everyone crammed in like cattle, and the trip to Australia is a complete nightmare altogether. Our daughter wants us to go over and Mary's keen to go, but you're not getting me sitting bolt upright for twenty odd hours to the ends of the earth. I'd rather stay at home and sleep in my own bed.

That's good now. We're ready to go. Oh, here comes Mary with the flask of tea. I told her we could buy tea out, but no, nothing would do but to send me off to the shed at eleven o'clock last night to find the flask we took on that trip to Galway, must have been twenty years ago, or even more, now that I think about, I think Haughey was still Taoiseach when we went to Galway. Anyway, here it is now and we can get going. Have I the shopping list? Yes. Driving glasses? Raincoat? Check, isn't that what you would say? Well, off we go then, let's hit the road, as they say, and no shilly-shallying.

Cuckoo

Peter looked closely at his reflection in the mirror as he trimmed his beard. He opened the bathroom door wide so that he could hear the sounds of the house. He could hear Ellen preparing his breakfast, and the baby banging his spoon on the tray of the high chair. He checked there were no hairs between his eyebrows, and then examined his sideburns for greying. Not yet. He stretched to his full height and surveyed himself. You'll do, he thought.

He heard the phone ringing and Ellen hurrying to answer it, then the murmur of her voice. He looked down at the bits of hair trimming in the sink, and opened the cabinet to find some aftershave, which he was used to patting on his cheeks, just for the luxury of the smell.

'Peter', Ellen called. He pushed aside a medicine bottle and a tin of talcum powder. She's moved everything again, he thought in mild irritation. 'Peter', he heard her call, looking in the study and then the bedroom. 'Oh, there you are,' she said as she appeared at the bathroom door.

'Where's my aftershave?' he asked

'I've got Susan on the phone,' she said.

'Why are you whispering?' he said. 'You can put that thing on mute you know, instead of clutching it like that'.

Ellen stood in the door holding the receiver close to her chest. 'It's Susan', she said, 'she wants to come and stay for a couple of weeks.'

Peter rolled his eyes to the heavens and went back to rummaging in the cabinet.

'What will I tell her?' Ellen asked.

'For God's sake, Ellen', he hissed, 'I'm going to work in a minute. What do I care what you do with your mad sister.'

Ellen backed away and lifted the receiver to her ear. 'That would be lovely, Susan. Tuesday, yes, the evening train. Peter'll pick you up at the station.' She said with a quick, silent appeal to her husband, who rolled his eyes again, but did not refuse. 'I must get back to the baby, but we'll look forward to seeing you on Tuesday. I'll have the spare room all ready for you'

'How long is she here for?' he asked when she had hung up. 'Fighting with Brian again, I suppose?'

Peter followed his wife to the kitchen and sat down to his breakfast. 'Haven't you done the toast yet?' he said.

'It's right here, darling,' said Ellen, rushing to the table with the toast. The baby looked at Peter with some interest and then continued banging his spoon.

'A couple of weeks she said. Brian is away on business, so it was a nice chance for a break and a catch up.'

'She should get a job of her own, lounging around the house all day or playing tennis with 'the girls'. I don't know how he puts up with her,' said Peter. 'All she thinks about is her appearance, and spending money on clothes.'

'Peter, you hardly know them. You only met them once, at the wedding,' said Ellen

'That was enough. Decked out like a Christmas tree, she was'.

'I thought she looked lovely,' said Ellen

Peter leaned over and gave her a peck on the cheek. 'I only had eyes for you,' he said. 'I don't like the flashy type. I'm off. Be back about six. Don't forget my dry cleaning.'

He drove to the station on Tuesday evening and collected Susan while Ellen got the dinner ready. He raised an amused eyebrow at the amount of luggage she hauled off the train. 'I didn't know you were moving in,' he joked, as he crammed her case and bags into the boot.

'Don't worry, Peter', she laughed, 'just a couple of weeks. How's Ellen and little

Adam? You're not working her too hard are you?'

'Not too much work involved in caring for your family,' he

replied. This was going to be a long fortnight, he could tell. She was getting at him already.

Ellen was delighted to see her sister and admired her hair and her jeans. 'And you're so lovely and slim. I'm still struggling to get back into the clothes I wore before Adam was born.' she said

'You know what Wallis Simpson said', Susan laughed, 'you can never be too rich or too thin? I'm still working on the rich.'

'I have some contracts to read up for tomorrow's meeting,' said Peter and went and locked himself in his study.

'How's his job going?' asked Susan. 'Didn't you tell me he was having trouble with his boss?' She picked at the cheese Ellen had grated for the pasta. 'Don't cook anything for me, sweetie, I'm trying to get rid of these last two pounds I put on over winter.'

'Are you sure? You must eat something. No, he changed his job a couple of months ago. Didn't I tell you? He's doing really well and the managing director is taking a real interest in his work. Looks like he'll be in line for a promotion soon. He says the sales manager they've got there now hasn't got a clue.'

'Don't they mind him having that beard? A lot of people are funny about hairy-faced men. It looks a bit grubby, don't you think, all that hair on your face? Well, no I don't suppose you do.'

'Oh, no, I think Peter looks very distinguished. I like his beard. It was probably the first thing I noticed about him, and those lovely blue eyes.'

'Hmm,' said Susan. 'I must go and shower and change. I had to sit next to this ghastly woman and her baby on the train. I'm sure the brat wiped its hands on my shirt.'

The two sisters always enjoyed their time together, shopping and drinking lattes and admiring cakes they had no intention of eating. The weather was glorious the next day, for a change, and they lay out in the garden soaking up the sunshine. When Peter came home from work, harried and hot, Susan greeted him cheerily, 'Hard day at the office, Peter? Taken over the firm yet?'

'Sit down here, Pete,' said Ellen, 'I'll get you a nice cold beer.'

'Must your sister parade herself around in next to nothing in front of everyone?' he asked Ellen later when they were in bed.

'I suppose,' she said, 'when you look that good in a bikini you might as well flaunt it. And the back yard is hardly a public place now, is it darling? Did you see how well she gets on with Adam? Gave him his breakfast this morning'

'Behind a full length overall, I don't doubt.' He grumbled. 'Can't see Lady Susan getting a spot of cereal on her designer clothes.'

The following evening Susan insisted on cooking dinner, and came back from the store laden with food. 'It's the least I can do,' she said over Ellen's protests.

'Peter just likes plain food.' Ellen warned.

'What about what you like?' asked Susan, 'no good letting them get all their own way, you know. They think they can boss you around if you act like a doormat. You need to stand up for yourself a bit.'

'I'm easy to please, really,' said Ellen, 'and I don't like to make a fuss. Peter's very good. He works hard to provide for his family, and I like looking after him.'

Susan laid the table in the dining room, instead of the kitchen where they usually ate, and put linen napkins and candles on the table. 'It looks really beautiful,' said Ellen, 'I hope Adam doesn't mess up your lovely tablecloth.'

'Oh, Ellen, pet, could we have just the grownups tonight? It'd be so nice, just us, maybe later when Adam is asleep.'

'I don't know, Susan,' said Ellen, 'Peter likes us to eat together, and he doesn't really like his meal too late. Upsets his stomach, he says. Oh, well', she said, seeing Susan's disappointment, 'I'm sure it won't matter this once. Yes, that would be lovely. I'll feed Adam in the kitchen and we'll dine in style later.'

Peter peered suspiciously at the food Susan prepared, but did not make any comment, even eating mushroom soup, much to Ellen's surprise, as she had understood he was allergic to mushrooms. The evening went well, the wine flowed freely and the candles softened the light and the atmosphere. Susan seemed happy and Peter was relaxed. Ellen was well pleased with the evening and glad she had put Adam to bed before dinner.

'What was that thing she cooked?' said Peter, peeling off his clothes and throwing them on the chair in the bedroom.

'Moussaka,' said Ellen, ' nice wasn't it?'

'And what was that purple stuff in it?'

'Aubergine.'

'Not bad, I suppose,' he said as he headed for the shower.

During the next few days Susan had eased up on the teasing, apart from a final salvo at Peter's beard, 'Hiding a weak chin, there, are you Peter?'

'Certainly not,' he bristled.

'I think the beard suits him,' said Ellen. 'His father had a beard and it stayed dark long after his hair had gone grey. Very distinguished.'

'Must have looked like a badger,' Susan mumbled, but hostilities seem to have eased during the second week of her stay. As Ellen was preparing dinner on Friday evening, and feeding Adam, she could hear them on the patio. She enjoyed the sound of the gentle clink of glasses and the soft hum of conversation and laughter coming through the French windows. I'm so relieved, she thought, I didn't think they'd get on at all. She suddenly realised how tense she had been since Susan had arrived, and thought back to her childhood when she was constantly in the shadow of her glamorous older sister, who, she must admit, had intimidated her for years. She smiled to herself, I can relax now, she thought, I didn't notice how worried I was that Peter and Susan wouldn't hit it off. Peter is not exactly the life and soul of the party and I suppose Susan can be a bit over the top.

'Dinner's nearly ready,' she called. 'I'll just put Adam to bed.'

'Oh, let's have it out here,' said Peter, 'it's a beautiful evening.' And she served the dinner al fresco. They sat late listening to the night sounds and making easy conversation. Ellen was the first to head for the bedroom, and she felt Peter slip into the bed beside her as she was drifting off to sleep.

On Saturday morning Peter liked to lie in and read the paper in bed. Susan went for an early swim, and Ellen enjoyed her morning with Adam and her routine.

Later in the morning when Adam was down for his nap, she stood rinsing his dish at the kitchen sink, looking out on the garden, her favourite view. Susan came through the back gate and walked across the grass in her bare feet, wriggling her toes in the soft dampness of an early morning shower. Her footprints trailed through the moist grass. A sound made her look up toward the house and Ellen saw her smile. She noticed Peter standing on the top step.

'Morning, darling,' Ellen called, 'Morning Susan. Isn't it a lovely day?'

Susan turned to look at her and waved. Peter turned his head towards the window at the sound of her voice. There was still the smile he had given Susan on his face, but his beard was gone.

Lithgow Station

Slight breeze, tap dripping
In the water cooler.
Old, tired plant pot hanging under the stairs
With its parched geranium.

Youngish tramp, worn and soiled
Asleep on a bench,
Her back turned to the tracks.

Drink machine broken, waiting room echoes,
Timetable empty, notice board blank.
Yesterday's rain trickling down the embankment;
Three linesmen down the track in orange jackets.

An old man, his shoes agape
For his swollen feet to breathe,
Feeds pastry from his meat pie
To a wary pigeon.
But a sparrow hops in
To steal the crumbs
From under the far seeing, unseeing eyes.

A goods train, thirty carriages long
Bellowing through, almost life.

Now the passenger train, on time this time
Disgorging bags, packs, cases, mail, people.
I crane my neck to look for mine.

THE MATCH

SATURDAY MORNING early John slipped out of bed and crept down the stairs, not to wake his grandparents. He knew which creaking steps to avoid, and he also knew to hurry because his grandfather would be up soon to let out the chickens.

He eased the back door open enough to slip through, and pulled his thin coat close as the morning chill met him. He set off along the hedgerow, and started collecting kindling for the fire. Small broken branches from the beech and ash trees were easy enough for him to break, but wrestling with the stubborn furze bushes for a few prickly twigs made his job take longer than he wanted. He hoped to have the fire set and lit and the kettle on the hob before his grandfather was up. He filled a bucket with kindling and headed to the rear of the shed for turf. When he went back into the kitchen he gathered a few sheets of newspaper and carefully twirled them into spills to light the fire. He stumbled into a chair hurrying to take the ashes out to the pile his grandfather had started a few weeks ago. A good pile of ash was always ready in the corner of the shed by this time of the year. Soon now it would be time to lift the bulk of the turnips and store them in the shed, out of the frost. They would keep well in a dry heap. They would keep even better with a light covering of sand, but ash would do fine. It was his job, after they had been lifted, to cut off the tops and be sure to leave a few turnips in the ground for the green tops later in the winter and in spring when food from the field was scarce.

Soon he had the fire lit and by the time the old man trudged down the stairs, the kettle was beginning to hiss. His grandfather nodded to him as he entered the kitchen, glanced at the fire and went outside to let the chickens out of the coop. John could hear his grandmother moving about upstairs, shuffling a little now as he listened, and pausing to rest more frequently than she used to. When he heard her start down the stairs, he quickly rinsed the teapot to warm it as she had taught him, put three spoons of tea in it from the caddy on the mantelpiece and had the tea wet before she got to the bottom of the stairs.

'You're a good boy, John,' she smiled and pulled her black cardigan around her thin shoulders. 'It's getting cooler now, the nights will be drawing in soon,' she said as she reached into the cupboard for the cups and the jug of milk. 'Will you make the porridge? Do you remember how it's done?'

'I do, of course,' said John and reached for the pan and the oats.

They worked quietly for a few minutes before John cleared his throat and said, 'There's a match on tomorrow, Nan. Did you know?'

'I thought I heard Ned say that to your grandfather right enough,' she said, 'when he brought that letter from Boston here yesterday.'

They were quiet for a few minutes more, John fussing over the fire and his grandmother examining the sugar to know would there be enough for the tea s well as the porridge. A letter from Boston always created tension in the house, sending his grandfather off on one of his harangues about his own son who had landed John on their doorstep ten years ago, soon after his wife had died in childbirth along with the new baby.

'I'll be back for the boy when I have a few bob made,' Dennis had said. He went to Boston to work and nothing had come from him since, bar the odd letter. No money for John's keep, nor any mention of taking the boy over to be with him. The letter they got in the spring said that he was to be married again to a girl from Sligo he had met over there.

His grandfather roared and shredded the latest letter and flung it in the fire. John had been outside but had heard the outburst and knew where the letter would have ended up. No chance now of reading it.

The old woman moved around the table setting out bowls and spoons while John stirred the porridge.

'Do you think he'll let me go?' he asked.

'What's that, Pet?'

'The match. Do you think he'll let me go?'

'I'll have a word, John. Don't get your hopes up now, but God is good.'

Soon they sat down to breakfast and Timmy listed the jobs that had to be done for the day. 'I want you,' he said to John, 'to pile up the earth around the leeks down the back of the acre. They're no good if the stems aren't blanched.' He looked over his glasses at the bent head of the boy in front of him. John was rapidly spooning porridge into his mouth. 'Don't gollop, boy,' his grandfather said. 'When God made time he made plenty of it.'

'Will I gather up the apples first, Pa?' The last of the apples had to be picked before the cold weather set in in earnest, then boxed up and stored on the earth floor in the shed. He had already picked the few remaining pears the day before and had laid them out, carefully separated, on newspaper under his bed, to ripen in the drier atmosphere of the house.

'No, boy, do the leeks first. We'll need to plant cabbage for the spring, too. I'll start that and you can help me when you've finished with the leeks. The apples can wait till this evening'

John drained his teacup and threw a beseeching look at his grandmother before he put on his work boots that had been drying near the fire. He put on his cap and went out, hunched against the rising wind.

'Look at the cut of him,' grumbled his grandfather, 'Will he ever be good for a day's work?'

'He's a grand lad, Timmy, and very willing. You're too hard on him. Isn't he only a boy'

'I was working a full six days a week at his age instead of sitting in a classroom in the warm all day. The sooner he learns you have to work for everything in this life the better. Maybe if you hadn't mollycoddled his father so much he wouldn't be taking his responsibilities so lightly now.'

'Dennis will be doing the best he can. They don't be having such an easy time of it in America either, Timmy.'

'He should have sent for the boy years ago. How long does he expect me to keep working to put a roof over his brat's head.'

'Shush, Timmy. He'll hear you. He's a good young one and it's not his fault if his father hasn't been able to get a home for him over there yet,' she soothed.

'Kicking up his heels in Boston, you mean,' said Timmy, roughly stuffing tobacco into his pipe.

He smoked quietly for a few minutes while Sarah got the bowl and flour and started making the bread. When she decided he would say no more for now, she said, 'John has a match tomorrow.' The old man grunted softly and knocked his pipe out on the side of the chimney.

Sunday morning John rose early again to set the fire, while the clouds were gathering. The small family sat down to boiled eggs and bread and butter for breakfast and Sarah had taken care to get Timmy's eggs just right, and John put four spoons of tea in the pot, to be sure the tea was good and strong, the way his grandfather liked it. He gave a questioning look to his grandmother but she just shook her head slightly to indicate she had no answer.

Timmy went outside and John followed him and watched him eagerly as he consulted the sky.

'Looks like it might be a good day, after all,' said John.

Timmy shrugged his bent shoulders and gazed up at the clouds. 'I don't know' he said, looking along the lines of turnips. 'If it keeps fine this morning....' he trailed off and shrugged again. He had lost some height with age. When John stood in front of him now they spoke eye to eye, but then John had grown rapidly in this last year.

'Will I hitch up the trap, Pa?' he said and watched his grandfather carefully for the answer, which could be the slightest twitch of an eyebrow.

'Unless you're planning to make your grandmother walk to Mass,' said the old man and trudged away towards the shed.

With the tub trap hitched, the old pony clopped at a sedate pace toward the church a mile and a half away, a path she knew without prompting. The clouds were holding off well enough, a good day for the match. John sat behind his grandmother to avoid the smoke swirling back from Timmy's pipe but he knew his eyes would be smarting from the fumes by the time they reached the chapel. They passed the next house along the way, and the boy counted the dahlias outside their front wall, just to amuse himself. His grandfather snorted in the direction of the neighbour's small garden. He never, he often said, saw any point in growing something that neither man nor beast could eat. The blackberries along the road were all gone by now, and the bushes had taken on a coating of dust from the passing carts and tractors. It had been a dry autumn so far.

Back at the house Sarah started preparing the dinner while John rubbed down the pony and put her in her stall with feed. After they had eaten Timmy sat by the fire and smoked his pipe. Sarah cleared away the dishes from the meal and John fidgeted quietly in the far corner half looking at a schoolbook and half watching his grandfather for a sign. When Timmy finished his pipe and knocked the bowl on the chimney to clear the ash, John straightened and waited. Timmy got to his feet slowly, stretched his back and sat again to take off his shoes and replace them with his work boots. John's shoulders slumped and he closed the book. He had his sign. The weather was good enough for lifting turnips.

What are the Odds?

It must have been midday when they put us in the boat. At least that's what Sean said. 'The sun is at its zenith.' That's the way he talks, throwing big words around. He is studying under Professor Olwyn Richards, fresh from Monash University, Melbourne. This experiment is her pet project. Four of us – desperately poverty stricken students that is – get to be stranded on an island for a month for a study in technological deprivation. She is testing the hypothesis that a reduction in interference from technology will facilitate memory function. She believes that 21st century western culture is eroding people's survival mechanisms through excessive reliance on technology. A recent survey has shown, according to Sean, that twenty year olds are far less able to remember simple things like telephone numbers than sixty year olds because the younger people rely on their mobile phones, computers, and stuff, whereas older people are more used to relying on their memories. Ergo, (I'm beginning to sound like him) isolating us on an island without our gizmos is supposed to support her theory. Penelope, the fourth member of this merry band is an anthropology major so presumably is just interested in the rest of us as animals in an experiment. I suppose we should be grateful they don't put us in cages. Mind you, when you think about it, four of us on a small island will probably feel like prison.

Sean is a psychologist, doing his doctorate in behavioural science; Eric is working on his sociology masters; me, I'm just a lowly undergraduate, hoping to get a half way decent computer science degree, so I can get a job, and finally make some money. And I play cricket. These other three act as if the only bat they ever heard of is one that lives in a tree and flies around at night.

Money is the only reason I'm here, for the generous allowance we are being given for our participation in this experiment, and the even more generous wad we get if we get our sums right. An additional carrot comes in the form of a bonus for whichever one of us gets the highest scores. A month out of my life just now is neither here nor there. I haven't been able to get a job for the summer and I could use some work on my tan. That and I need to be around in case I have to repeat in September, which I have to tell you, is quite on the cards. I like to play hard and party hard, and my tutor is a sadistic slave driver.

Three men and one girl. Maybe the test is one of those where they tell you it is about one thing and it's really about something else. Maybe they are actually watching to see if the three guys will kill each other over the girl. Well, folks I'm here to tell you, this is not going to happen; Lady Penelope is in no danger from yours truly. That's all I'm going to say.

So they've taken our watches, computers, mobile phones and anything else that looks remotely like a gadget, which is why presumably we have to suffer Sean's superior skills in reading the sky, as if the world and his dog don't know that it's midday when the sun is right up there.

The idea of an island was to emphasise our isolation, as was the symbolic voyage over water. I bet the project name is Gilligan or something equally creative. It didn't take long to get to the island, the boat trip itself was uneventful except it was already obvious that the three eggheads were going into a huddle whenever they could and not taking kindly to the sportsman, me, out on deck miming his batting technique. Like air guitar for Freddie Flintoff. The people from the psychology department had set up everything for us in the way of accommodation, food etc. and there was a roster so we couldn't fight about whose turn it was to put out the cornflakes. No entertainment, obviously. Not part of the deal. We had a look around when we landed, and then sort of moped for a while, nobody not quite sure what to do next. It was like Big

Brother without the cameras. Little brother maybe, I said to Eric who looked at me as if I was something unpleasant he had just trodden on.

So here's the thing. When I signed up for the experiment I was given a whole barrage of psychometric tests. I was tested on cognitive function, storing and retrieving chunks of numbers in my memory; storing and retrieving lists of words, symbols, and pictures. They gave me personality tests, Myers-Briggs profiling, neurolinguistic programming stuff, and, so help me one of those lie detector tests. Now I know what a galvanic skin response is. That's going to be useful in Silicon Valley, when Bill Gates beckons. My scores were recorded and the purpose and methods of the test explained to me. They even asked me my reason for volunteering for the experiment. They could have put the polygraph on me then OK, because I told the truth and nothing but the truth. I needed the money to see me through the summer till my old man coughed up my allowance in the autumn. And it wouldn't do any harm on my CV either.

My three amigos were there for knowledge, furthering their understanding of their own cognitive processes, assisting the course of scientific research blah, blah, blah. That's what they told me when we met up for the first time, trying to make out they didn't care about the money or the competition. What I had in common with those three losers I couldn't imagine, and they seemed just as mystified, obviously regarding me as some kind of muscle-bound low life.

Before we were accepted for the experiment we had to sign an agreement to abide by the rules of the test and not try to smuggle in stuff like mobile phones. We all signed up, but they still went through our bags to check that we hadn't smuggled any contraband. It was like going through customs, with the X ray machine and the patting down. Lady Penelope was furious, and protested at the lack of trust. Perhaps she was frightened she was going to be strip-searched. She should be so lucky. Eric stood to attention, very grand, looking far above it all, and you could see Sean was taking mental notes to include in his own journal publications later. Me, I put a key in my pocket, just to give them the excitement of finding something.

Now I told you I was in IT, so all jokes aside I knew I was going to find it hard with not a keyboard or screen in sight for a whole month. No texting, no gaming, no DVDs, no emails, no sneak look at porn sites. No television, not even a book to read. But I came prepared. I had a tennis racket, a basketball, a cricket bat, golf clubs, runners and other sports gear. They wouldn't let me bring my pedometer. What did the trio from Science Monthly have? Notebooks, pencils, pens, tippex, paper clips and who knows what else, to record their observations. OK so I had a notebook and a pen too, which is why I'm writing this, just for something to do, not that I'm going to hand it in at the end, for reasons you will discover later. We have to give a brief verbal report when it's all over but there will be no more tests, lie detector or otherwise. The monitoring of the changes, or not, in our learning processes will be done on an ongoing basis. Each day each one of us is given an identical set of figures and words that we must memorise. The lists would be brought by boat every morning in sealed envelopes by one of Olwyn's flunkies, who would have taken away the previous days' test papers and the rubbish, and brought back the previous day's results, toothpaste, aspirins, food, whatever else we might need that doesn't take batteries. We were not allowed to speak to the person on the boat. Every evening at 8.00 we took turns at going into the isolated room at the back of the house where the professor, or one of her minions, phoned us up and ran through the test questions for that day. There are four of us, a pretty small sample but we can monitor each other, and snitch on anyone who is cheating or colluding. They have explained that, obviously, colluding or helping each other in any way is a no-no, but they are confidant that their methods are cheat proof. But they have figured without Bat Boy. I know my way around computers and I have my own little scam going.

We'd get our assignment in the morning and then scatter to the four corners of the island to swat up for the test in the evening. I found the perfect little hideaway, a narrow bay as far away from the cabin as possible, where I could practice my batting, or work on my slice or throw a few hoops in peace, and the weather was perfect.

After day four the three wise monkeys were looking at me rather differently. When the results came every morning and there was a clear winner, their superior sneers were being replaced by curiosity and something I'd like to think looked like respect. I was knocking them dead; they couldn't understand how this alien being from the planet 'normal' could do better than a bunch of no-life nerds. Well, this is how. Before we left I hacked into the computer and accessed the tests that were prepared for us for the month. Nothing to it. With all the answers at my fingertips I could make a killing with minimum effort, win every day and earn myself a nice little stash in the process. Nothing stupid, no perfect scores, no flaunting my lack of study, just quietly filling in my days and wearing the same worried look as they did when I went to do the test every evening.

I know what you're thinking. How could I have smuggled in all the answers when we were searched before we got on the boat? Our luggage, our person, they practically looked in our mouths? T-shirts are the answer, simple, ordinary, T-shirts. I downloaded all the answers and printed them onto the inside of tee shirts. I used a couple of dozen of them to give me plenty of changes of clothes, and mixed up the sequence of answers so I could ring the changes. I'm not stupid enough to wear the same shirt every day, or just swap the same two T-shirts all the time, and couldn't risk washing them as the printing would come off in the machine. All I had to do when I went into the isolation room was whip off my shirt, turn it inside out, read the answers, get a couple wrong, put it back on and walk out with a relieved look on my face.

By the end of the first week the two guys hated my guts, I could tell. They were being beaten at their own game by what they obviously considered to be an inferior being. We avoided each other whenever possible. Penelope though, or Penny, as she invited me to call her, seemed suddenly to notice I was alive, and find my company fascinating. At least her taste was improving. She was turning out to be a sweetheart, and got better looking every day. One day she did all my rostered chores for me so that I could 'study in peace' as she put it. Another day she turned up a pair of jeans for me. This girl was eating out of my hand. I still took off after breakfast for most of the day, but Penny and I had some quality time in the afternoons and evenings, if you know what I mean. If this experiment really turned out to be about two guys killing the one who got the girl, I'd need to watch my back! But really, Eric and Sean were totally eaten up by being beaten at the tests. One day I even caught them going through my things to see if I had the answers tucked in the bottom of my bag or thrown in with my socks. Even if I hadn't found them poking around my room, their feeble attempts to put my stuff back where I'd thrown it would have given them away. Even ransacking someone's room they couldn't help being neat freaks. I decided to have a bit of fun with them after that, and started to go without my revision papers in the mornings, just picking them up off the table with a bored yawn after lunch. I could see it was choking them.

Over a week in and I was king of the island, scoring with the test and with the girl. Life was peachy. I could hear the tinkle of the cash as I hit the jackpot.

After lunch on day eight I picked up my test papers and went off to my room to 'study'. Penny followed me. I opened the door, walked in and stopped dead in my tracks. When she saw the look of horror on my face, she backed away, ' What's the matter?' she whined in that stupid voice of hers, I thought you'd be pleased. I cleaned up your room and sent most of your clothes back with the boat to be laundered.'

The Queen

It was a June day in London, and teaming with rain. Katie wiped the condensation from the inside of the bedroom window with the side of her hand, and peered out at the back garden. The stakes propping up the few runner beans her father had planted were bent low by the wind, and the wild rose, trying to hide the broken fence, drooped its head in submission to the downpour.

Katie turned back to her sister who was trying to make the bed. Every time she lifted the sheet in the air the cat ran under it. They were both enjoying the game and Katie looked on delighted. Making the bed was always near impossible when the cat was there, and when she wasn't, one of the girls would go looking for her to enjoy their morning game. When the sheet was finally in place Susan started to lift up the blanket. 'You could help me,' she hissed at her sister.

'She'll get soaked if they leave the carriage open. Do you think they'll leave the carriage open?' Katie asked.

'Of course they won't, silly. Who wants a drowned rat for a queen.'

'But then nobody will be able to see her if the lid is up,' said Katie.

'It's not a lid. It's a roof. You have a lid on a sardine tin, not a gold carriage. And anyway, we won't be seeing her, so I don't care.'

'Is it really a golden coach? Isn't gold really, really heavy? Will the horses be hurt?' asked Katie still gazing at the rain beating down on a commuter train passing close to the house. 'You know, horses will gallop till they drop dead, the queen would never kill her horses would she?' She sighed, 'I'd love to see the procession.'

She moved to the bed to help her sister with the heavy woollen blanket. They took a side each and raised it up in time for the cat to dive underneath and they both collapsed on the bed stifling their giggles. Soon Katie was caught under the blanket with the cat and Susan whispered urgently, 'Get out of there, Mum's coming.' Katie quickly jumped up, grabbed the cat and shoved it under the bed, and before Carol opened the door the two girls were standing each side of the bed quietly spreading the blanket and tucking the corners in as she had shown them.

'What's all that scuffling and giggling I can hear? What are you doing?' she demanded as she strode into the room, banging the door against the small dressing table behind it.

The sisters offered innocent, flushed faces and said, in unison, 'Nothing, Mummy.'

Carol sighed and turned to the younger girl and said, 'Leave that for now. I want you to go and get some milk for your father's breakfast, and then you'll have to go up to the shop pick up the battery for the radio. I want to listen to the Coronation.'

Katie raced down the stairs, delighted to have dodged the bed making, while Susan finished the bed, mopped the floor and shook their small, threadbare mat out of the window, a job that had to be done every day, rain or no rain.

After they had finished breakfast and the girls were washing the dishes Len, their father's work mate, arrived. The two men ran a small business renovating houses, many of them still war damaged, or they erected prefabricated housing for the council.

'No work today, Len,' said their father Dave, 'we're taking the girls to see the Coronation.' Katie nearly dropped the plate she was drying. The sisters shared a delighted, silent dance. This was much better than they could have hoped for.

Carol shot a surprised, sullen look at her husband, but made no comment. She was sitting at the corner of the kitchen table carefully applying red polish to her nails. Len looked from one to another and then made himself comfortable at the kitchen table, helping himself to tea and rattling the last out of a packet of arrowroot biscuits. The girls put away the dishes as Dave polished his best shoes. 'Might as well have a day off', he said as Len nodded agreement, 'the girls'll enjoy seeing the Coronation procession. Shame about the rain.'

'Oh, we don't mind,' said Susan quickly, afraid he might change his mind. 'Can we put on our new dresses?' she asked.

'No,' said Carol, without looking up from her nails, ' you can wear your school uniform. No need for a fashion parade. I don't imagine Queen Elizabeth will be craning her neck out of the coach to see what you two are wearing. Those dresses are for best and I won't have them ruined in this weather.'

As her daughters raced off, Carol also went to change, while Dave and Len sat smoking at the table. When she returned both men looked at her, Dave whistled softly and Len looked quickly back down at his cigarette.

'You look like a queen yourself,' said Dave.

'Just because we have to live in a dump doesn't mean I have to go around in rags,' said Carol and tossed her head to release her long hair from the collar of her coat.

They battled their way through thousands of people near Marble Arch to catch a glimpse of the new queen. Nearly three million people lined the streets of London in the torrential rain. The sisters took turns climbing on Dave's shoulders to get a better look at the coaches going by, or peering through a makeshift periscope that street peddlers were selling by the hundreds to people too far back to see over the heads of the crowds. Most of the carriages had their roofs rolled up and the onlookers had to be guided by the program and anonymous hands, waving from the windows, to work out who were the famous people they had come to see. The Coronation coach glistened like a golden monochrome rainbow. The roof was closed, but there were big windows on each side for the royal couple to wave through. A huge cheer went up when it appeared. The only other coach that raised the crowd's sodden spirits was the one carrying the queen of Tonga. Queen Salote Tupuo had never been heard of in Britain before the royal visit to Tonga earlier in the year, and the crowd was curious to see this larger than life woman who reigned over a people who had only recently, according to the press, given up their traditional practice of cannibalism. When Princess Elizabeth had visited Tonga, Queen Salote herself held a huge umbrella over her visitor's head to protect her from a sudden shower. Today she refused to let them cover her coach and she stood waving to the crowd, ignoring the deluge. The cheer she got was nearly as loud as that for the Queen Elizabeth. Her husband Tungi Mailefihi was barely visible beside her. Michael MacLiammoir later told the story that while they were watching the parade, someone asked, as the Tongan carriage passed, 'Who's that little chap with Queen Salote?' to which Noel Coward promptly replied, 'Probably her lunch.'

Susan and Katie were wet, dirty but ecstatic by the time they set off for home. The weather was clearing and the street party was still to come. They struggled through tents and blankets; food and clothing abandoned by the hordes who had camped through the night to get a good view of the parade. As the family tramped back to the tube station, the girls played a game of seeing who could spot the most discarded toys among the debris. Dave amused himself by spearing oranges and apples on the point of his umbrella, and Carol walked, tight lipped, a few paces in front of her husband and children ignoring the detritus around her feet.

Their own street was decorated with streamers and lined with trestle tables with white tablecloths. Most of the mothers, and some of the fathers and grandmothers served the children sandwiches and jelly and rock cakes. They had bread with hundreds and thousands sprinkled on top, toffee apples, which had only recently been taken off rationing, and nougat, which no one could pronounce, and liquorice laces. A man with a microphone led the cheers for the young, beautiful queen and her husband, Prince Phillip, and another loud, excited cheer, especially from the boys, for Edmund Hilary who had reached the peak of Everest only a few days before.

Katie wrapped a piece of cake, two cheese sandwiches and some fairy bread in a napkin and took them into the house for her parents, dripping nonpareils all the way up the stairs. In the kitchen she found her mother sitting at the corner of the kitchen table in her damp new suit, drumming her fingers on the table and staring vacantly out of the window. Dave came into the room. He had changed from his good clothes and put on his second best suit. 'Think I might go down to the Red Lion and have a pint,' he said.

'Naturally,' said Carol without turning her head.

Later Katie staggered up the stairs with a plate of treacle pudding and custard, breathlessly announcing that there were going to be games, and some of the children were in fancy dress. 'I sat next to a bride and a jockey, and one boy was done up as Bangers and Mash. Mummy, you should come down, the races are starting in a minute, and there are prizes.' As she spoke they heard Len's step on the stairs followed by a fluttery scrape on the door, hardly a knock at all. He poked his head around the door and asked, 'Dave home?'

'He's gone to the pub,' said Katie, 'and Mummy's coming down to the party.'

'I don't think I'll be able to,' said Carol. 'I've got a terrible headache. I think I must have caught a cold in all that rain.' She passed a weary hand across her brow.

'How about I make a nice cuppa?' asked Len and filled the kettle without waiting for an answer.

Katie headed for the door and her mother called after her, 'I think I'll have to take an aspirin and lie down, so be quiet when you come back in, and tell your sister too. I don't want you both clattering up the stairs all day.'

All the children in the street were given a presentation book, a cup and spoon with the queen's picture on it. The two girls laughed themselves sick at the three-legged race when they fell in a heap, just yards from the finish line. Then Susan won the 100 yards race for her age and was awarded a commemorative pint glass. She raced off to show her mother, who was still sitting at the kitchen table drinking tea with Len. The gifts and prizes were piled up on the table, surrounded by cake and sweets and silly hats.

'No more noise, thank you, Susan, and no more food. I feel far too ill to eat. I'm going to have a rest' said Carol.

When Katie won her next race she was given a decorated, coronation pint glass as well and went quietly up the stairs with her prize. She was afraid it would get broken if she left it under her seat at the table. She remembered to make no noise, not to disturb her mother. The bedroom door was closed as she crept past. She reached across the kitchen table to place the glass carefully in the centre, where it would be safe, steadying herself against Len's coat on the back of the chair. The smell of his tobacco was still hanging in the air. Satisfied that her trophy was safe, she sped back to the street to find Susan. The egg and spoon race was next.

MORNING AFTER

'WAKE UP, Martin.'

His mother shook him vigorously. 'Wake up, the gardai are outside.' Martin grunted under the covers and turned over. 'The gardai are outside,' she repeated.

This roused him, and he peered blearily from under his pillow. 'What do they want?' he said.

'How do I know what they want, they're outside sitting in the car. What did you get up to last night? The racket you made coming in at all hours staggering up the stairs, it's a wonder you didn't bring them in with you.' She pulled the curtain back about an inch. Martin groaned and hid his head under the pillow. 'For pity sake, don't let the light in,' he said.

'One of them's writing in a book, and the other one's on the phone,' she reported. 'You'd better get up and go and see what they want. God help you if you've brought more trouble to this house.'

Martin emerged again, as his mother hurried out of the room. He groped around on the bedside table for a drink of water and his mobile phone. There was no water and he licked his lips to try to moisten them. He found the phone under the bed, and called his mate, Kevin. 'Kevin,' he whispered, 'did we do anything last night. You know, after we left the pub.'

'Go away, Clancy,' said Kevin, 'and let me die in peace,' and he cut the connection. A knock came on the front door. He flung himself out of the bed, grabbed trousers and a t-shirt from the floor, and staggered down the stairs.

At the door he raised bloodshot eyes to the officers standing there. 'Robert Kennedy?' demanded the nearest garda. Martin braced himself on the jamb of the door and waved feebly to the left. 'Next door,' he croaked.

Number Twenty-Eight

Kitty could feel the chill of the air through her thin nightdress. These days it took her longer to get going in the morning, her limbs were stiff, and when she put her feet on the floor to get out of bed, she had to push herself upright with her hands on the mattress. The first thing she always did was to pull on her dressing gown and kneel down, resting her elbows on the bed, to thank the Good Lord for bringing her through the night and to say a prayer for the soul of her husband, Jack. These days she needed to stretch and groan to ease the ache in her back before she could face the stairs. If it weren't for the chickens, some days she would be tempted to burrow down into the blankets and enjoy the warmth for a few more minutes.

Her daughter, Mary, who lived in New York, and telephoned every Sunday evening, said she should stay in bed in the warm and say her prayers before she got up, but Kitty felt that that would be disrespectful to the Lord.

She sighed, thinking of Jack; how the two of them had gone about their chores after he retired. Although he never had much to say it was good to have him there, and gave her a reason to cook a meal in the middle of the day. Often now she just made a pot of tea and had a bit of brown bread and some hard cheese; cheese and apple. 'A match made in heaven, Kitty,' Jack used to say, 'just like us'.

As she eased her way down the stairs she heard the cat calling her from the kitchen windowsill. Jack had never allowed him in the house but now she fed him in the kitchen and sometimes when she sat knitting in front of the television, he leapt up onto her lap and played with the wool and she pretended to scold him.

She acknowledged the Sacred Heart over the door on the landing, and headed for the kitchen to light the fire and put on the kettle. Jack was gone and her only child was a continent away but she took great comfort from her religion, and her parish priest, Father Gough, was always there with a kindly word.

She lifted the cloth off the bowl of mash she had prepared last night for the chickens; 'my girls' she called them to herself, but wouldn't dare to repeat that to Mary for fear of being laughed at. Every evening she squeezed the cooked potatoes and their skins with her hands. Kitty had never liked the way the potato oozed through her fingers like cold, pale worms, but she ignored her distaste because she knew that the hens enjoyed picking at their breakfast. If she had bread or vegetables, or meat scraps she would mix them in with the potato, and some eggshell, ground up very small because Jack had explained to her that if they knew they were eating shell, they would attack their own eggs. Finally she mixed in some rolled oats and a little milk. By the morning the mix was soft and the oats had swelled.

She had blocked out the sound of the chickens calling her, but now she stood at the sink and looked out towards their coop, which was attached to the back of the shed. As she looked, absently stirring the mash with a wooden spoon, she noticed that she had not closed the shed door properly; it stood so slightly ajar that she had to squint to be sure. She tried to remember when she was last in there. Jack was always telling her that she was too trusting, and he had put a padlock on the shed, although she never used it now. It was too stiff for her fingers to manage on a cold morning, and what was in there to steal anyway, a spade or two, some straw for the chickens and last year's Christmas decorations.

'I'll have my tea later,' she said to herself as the kettle boiled. She talked to herself a lot now, 'I'll check that door first.'

As she reached the shed door, she heard a faint scurrying inside, and opened the door wide, peering into the gloom. She nearly dropped the bowl of mash when she saw a small boy huddled in the far corner, blinking into the light. He jumped up and made to run past her, but she caught him by the shoulder and barred his way.

'What are you doing in my shed?' she demanded, 'there's nothing to steal here. I'll call the garda to you, and your mother.'

'I'm not a thief,' he spat back at her, 'get your stinking hands off me.'

'Not until you tell me what you're doing in my shed.'

The boy had his head bowed almost onto his chest, and she could not hear what he mumbled.

'Speak up, boy,' she said, not frightened now, but indignant.

'I was asleep.' The boy said clearer now, looking up, but not meeting her eyes.

'Asleep. In my shed? Whatever for?'

The boy sniffed and she could see that he was trying not to cry. 'Sit down on that bale of straw,' she said, 'and let me look at you.' He looked desperately at the door, but he could not have got out without knocking her down, so he reluctantly shuffled over to the straw and sat down. He had on a threadbare coat over a grubby shirt, and a cap that was two sizes too small for his head. His knees below the short trousers were dirty and grazed, and blue with the cold. At the end of his spindly legs he wore a pair of boots that were as big as the cap was small, with no sign of socks, but the chafing marks of the boots across his shins.

'I've never seen a boy so thin,' she said, 'what are you doing here? What's your name?'

He kept his head bowed, 'I'm a runner, missus, and I'm called 28.'

'Runner, 28? What are you talking about boy? 28 is no kind of a name, and what's a runner?' Alarm rose up in her again. Was he queer in the head?

He told her then, in a halting voice that he had run away from the local Industrial School. Some of the boys were always trying to escape, and he was one of them. The priest called them 'Runners' and most of them were caught again soon. 'But, I won't be caught this time,' he cried, showing more spirit than she had seen in him so far.

'And what did you do to get sent there?' she asked, 'a boy doesn't be sent to the Industrial School for no good reason.'

'There's boys there that stole things,' he explained, 'or some that ran away from home or school, but I had no one and they put me there to be minded. Minded!' he cried with disgust. 'They couldn't mind a cat.' He tried to stop speaking when he saw her purse her lips in disapproval, but the words came rushing out, 'Oh, they beat us, missus, something unmerciful, and worse.' She could not imagine what could be worse, but quickly said, 'It's their responsibility to chastise you when you misbehave.'

The boy gave her a scathing look, and said no more for a minute. Kitty had no idea what do to next. If she left him to call the authorities he would run, for sure. She could not bring herself to lock him in the shed. As she looked, as if for inspiration, into the bowl of mash she became aware that he, too, was eyeing the chicken's mash in the bowl.

She said softly, 'Are you hungry, boy?' and he nodded without speaking.

'Right then,' said Kitty, her mind made up, 'come into the kitchen with me and have something to eat. The chickens can wait a few more minutes.'

They sat at the kitchen as the boy ate and Kitty watched him. They did not speak. He hardly breathed as he stuffed food into his mouth. She gave him brown bread and butter and some cold bacon and a tomato. While he golloped that, she boiled two fresh eggs, and he downed them along with cups and cups of sweet tea. She found some of last year's blackcurrant jam and he piled that onto more bread and devoured everything, bending low to the table and darting his eyes about like an animal on the look out for attackers. Finally, he sighed and leaned back in the chair.

With more tea in front of them both, he began to talk. His real name was Jerry, Jerry Brown, but at the school they were never called by name, only by number and he had grown used to answering to 28. He was twelve years old and had been sent to the Industrial School when his mother died when he was eight.

'What happened to your father?' asked Kitty.

'He went on the drink, missus. Nobody knows where he is now.'

He shared a dormitory with seventy other pupils in a damp red brick building that was always cold. The first year, he told her, wasn't too bad, although they were always hungry, but then the beatings started.

Kitty's face took on that distant look she had the first time he mentioned the beatings. 'The priests and the brothers are only there for the good of the children. They're there to care for you all. I can't believe they would beat you for no good reason.' She was aware that she sounded prim and defensive, and Jerry refused to say more for some minutes. She decided to risk leaving him to feed the chickens, and when she came back in he was sitting, huddled beside the fire as if he could never get warm enough.

When she came in, he turned to her and said, 'I'm not lying to you. They said all the time that we were liars and would burn in hell for all eternity, but I'm only telling you the truth. They had this strap that they hit us with. It was two leather straps sewn together, with coins sewn in between them for strength and weight, and they'd strip you first and swing that strap, they didn't care where it landed. One lad nearly lost an eye. Why would I make that up?'

Kitty blessed herself, collapsing on the chair in distress and confusion. 'I don't know what to believe,' she muttered to herself, while the boys eyes bored into her, 'the priests would surely never do that.'

'Look,' he said suddenly and dragged off one of his filthy boots. Around the inside and outside of his ankles were old sores and the marks of welts. 'The priest over us hit me with the flat of his golf stick. He was mad for the game and carried a golf club with him everywhere so that he could practice his swing, and always have a weapon handy. The runners weren't allowed socks so that the boots would rub and the boots you got never fitted for the very same reason.'

'Where were you running to, if there's no one left at home?'

'I wanted to look for my father, and I couldn't stay there with those evil devils. I'd be better off in your shed, than back in that awful place. Don't send me back, missus,' he pleaded. 'I'll be out of your hair in a while.'

'But you have nowhere to go,' said Kitty and she twisted her wedding ring round and round her finger, an anguished look on her face.

She asked him if he wanted a bath, but he shrank back in horror, and she realised her mistake, remembering what he had told her about being stripped for the beatings. But he was glad enough for a bowl of warm, soapy water to soak his feet. They sat quietly; the only sound the occasional soft lapping of the water as Jerry wriggled his toes. The chickens grumbled contentedly outside the window. Kitty kept adding a little hot water to the bowl from the kettle on the hob, and the boy closed his eyes, the tightness leaching slowly out of his face.

'You could stop here,' she said suddenly, and her hand flew to her mouth as if to stop the words, but she blurted out, 'I could say you were my grandson, come over from New York to stay for a while.'

Jerry sat up straight and they exchanged shy, astonished smiles. They said nothing for long minutes.

'I can work, missus,' he said, 'It wouldn't cost you.'

They both looked up in alarm at a quiet knock at the back door, and before they could move the door opened and Father Gough's large frame darkened the opening.

'I just called, Mrs Crean, to see how...' His voice faded away as he saw the terrified face of the boy in front of him. He looked from Jerry to Kitty and back again.

'Ah,' he said, 'the runner. They've been looking all over for you my boy. You've set the school a merry dance. They're getting a bit tired of your nonsense. It was very good of you Mrs Crean to hold him.'

'But I didn't...' she started to say, as the boy shot her a glance full of despair and hatred.

'Dry your feet, boy', said Father Gough, throwing the youngster a towel from the back of the chair. 'Don't worry yourself, Mrs Crean. We'll soon have this miscreant back where he belongs.' As he dragged the boy out of the back door by his collar, she could hear the Angelus bell ringing, and she covered her ears.

Galvanised

For the first six months we lived
In the far end of the tin shed, hunched
Through winter
Over a paraffin heater
While they built the house.

Our breath made streaks of ice
On the morning blankets.
Corrugated misery, perpetual picnic.

There was a five inch gap between the wall and the roof.
In the wind the whole place rattled like
The tin can that it was.

Once I was sick and spent three days
In my neighbour's spare room.
I watched the house grow, slow
And wished I could have been sick more.

The Outdoor Setting

They heard the unmistakable sound of a car trailer rattling down the long dirt driveway, the wheels grinding on the dusty gravel road that led to their house. Kate had rented it for herself and her daughter a few months previously, and had deliberately chosen a basic, rural setting designed to calm their nerves. That was after she had decided that it was best for everyone to put an end to the marriage which had increasingly become fuelled only by animosity. The hostility between herself and Paul had leached like malignant fog from the bedroom, down the hall to the kitchen, all through the dining room, blocked out the television in the sitting room, contaminated the plants in the garden, despoiled the garage, driveway, dog; any happy thing in its path.

Out here in the scrub, Kate was beginning to relax. They could sit on the back patio in the evening and watch the sun that disappeared so suddenly over the hill opposite the creek at the bottom of their 'patch of the outback' as they liked to call it. An acre meant nothing to the sheep stations all around them, but to Kate and Vicki it was a haven where they could sometimes watch a wallaby bound through the twilight, or wonder what a flock of galahs could find to eat in the thin, dry patch of grass near the clothesline. The creek meant they could plant a few trees, mostly native varieties that would last better in the drought, which was searing its way towards them from the north. She bought a pump and pumped water up to the kitchen garden to water her precious apple trees, and Vicki grew lettuce and beetroot and marigolds. When their door was closed at night their world was quiet and calm, until a donkey in the village woke the cockerel at four thirty in the morning, who woke everyone else. Kate laughed when she described the peace and quiet of country life to her friends, and they all told her how well it suited her.

One day in early spring, in the middle of the lambing season, Vicki had come howling into the house that a magpie was attacking a lamb, just over the fence of the adjacent property. Kate phoned the homestead, leaving a message with the manager's wife that the bird was trying to peck out the eyes of the lamb, and the lamb and its mother were helpless and bleating. She and Vicki ran up and down the fence line shouting and flapping their hands to frighten the bird off, but the magpie eyed them with scorn and soon the lamb was lifeless and the sheep bawling, and no one had come.

Paul had been astonished and disbelieving when Kate had told him they were leaving, and briefly, before their departure, the rows had escalated. He would change, things would be good again. How could she deprive him of his daughter? What would he say to his parents? What the hell was the matter with her anyway? Vicki went to stay with him in town most weekends, and came home disgruntled and surly. 'Dad's lonely in the house all by himself, and his cooking's terrible. Why did we have to leave? Why can't he live out here with us?'

They heard the car and trailer pull up.' It's Dad,' cried Vicki, hanging out of the window and waving frantically.

Kate took a deep breath and pushed her meal aside. She walked to the door following her daughter, who had flung it wide in her rush to greet her father.

Paul got out of the car and embraced Vicki, looking over the top of her head at Kate, who stayed on the top step and had not spoken.

'You're all hot, Dad,' said Vicki,

' It's a fair old trip in this weather. No air conditioning in my old jalopy,' he said, not taking his eyes from her mother.

'Look what Dad's got,' Vicki cried, pointing to the wooden outdoor setting lashed to the trailer in an upright position, as if ready for a picnic.

Paul stepped forward, 'I've decided to give up the house,' he said, 'I thought you might as well have the garden setting. You remember how long it took me to make it? Vicki could have her breakfast in the garden.'

He looked around at the dry landscape. Kate remained on the step watching a young magpie, already as big as its parents, splashing in the feeble spray of a short hose under the apple tree. Getting big and strong to kill more lambs, Kate thought sourly, but did not shoo it away. Magpies will do what magpies will do, she thought, whether I like it or not.

Vicki climbed onto the trailer and started to tap dance on the tabletop, carefully watching her feet and shooting little glances at her mother.

'Look Mum, isn't it great?'

Kate still stood watching the bird, while its parents watched her.

When it was clear she was not going to answer, her husband turned towards her again, 'Where would Madam like it?' he asked with a mock bow in her direction.

'Over there, Dad, 'shouted Vicki, 'near where Mum's going to put the barbecue.'

'Bit near that hibiscus don't you think, eh Kate? What about here next to this tree at a bit of an angle to catch the shade?' said Paul.

Vicki jumped off the trailer, 'Great table, isn't it Mum? Isn't Dad clever, to make it himself.' Father and daughter stood together at the bottom of the steps, looking up at her, united in their enthusiasm.

The setting was identical to those found in public parks, the wood already turning grey from the weather. She closed her eyes for a moment, not wanting him there, not wanting the outdoor setting, not wanting to disappoint her daughter.

When she didn't reply Paul started undoing the ropes. 'Give us a hand to get it off the trailer then,' he said.

'Grab the seat, Mum, not the table part,' said Vicki.

'Why's that?'

'It's a special way we made them,' Paul explained, 'so that the top can come off when you move them. It's hardwood, the best, so it's pretty heavy. Clever idea isn't it?'

'Well, why don't we take the top off now, to move it?' she asked.

'No, no need. You two grab that side and old muscles with get this side. Where did you say you wanted it?'

'Near the barbecue,' said Vicki

'No, not a good spot' he said, 'not enough shade. Over here.'

Kate sighed and capitulated. 'Maybe the trailer could be brought closer,' she said.

'No, no it'll be right.' said Paul, and he nudged Vicki and winked at her, 'We're strong enough aren't we?'

'Course we are, Dad,' said Vicki pretending to flex her muscles.

Between them they lugged the setting off the trailer, and half dragged, half

carried it over to the place Paul had chosen.

'Perfect.' said Paul and sat down, miming impatience, with his knife and fork in the air. 'Where's the waiter in this place. Call itself five star.' Vicki giggled in delight and sat at the other side of the table, banging her fists and shouting, 'We want our dinner.'

Paul rubbed his hands together and looked around again.

'You don't go in for much gardening, do you? What I couldn't do with a place like this. Why don't I draw you up a plan, on graph paper, the real thing, just for the house garden?'

'We're managing fine, thank you,' said Kate stiffening.

Vicki stopped banging the top of the table. 'Can Dad stay the night?' she asked, out of the blue.

'Oh, I don't think that would be necessary, darling,' Kate said quickly. Paul looked down at the bird still fluttering under the sprinkler.

'Oh, Mum, he's had a long drive and it's late,' she wailed.

'Now Vicki, don't argue with your mother' said Paul, 'if she doesn't want me here she's allowed to make that choice.'

'Well, I'll go back with him then,' said the child, scowling. Paul got up and went to the trailer, and started winding the ropes he had used to tie the table down. The trailer would be even noisier going out empty. Kate stood with her hands hanging by her side willing herself not to wring them.

Vicki tried again, 'Can't he, Mum, just this once?'

Kate sighed, 'I suppose it wouldn't hurt this once.' Paul put the ropes in the boot and started to wind up the windows of the car, and slapped at a mosquito on his arm. Vicki did another little dance, on the grass this time, and ran to give her father another tight hug.

Kate turned off the hose and walked into the house. The magpie baby stopped flapping its wings and its parents moved closer, watching every move.

'Are you OK?' he asked he asked, looking down at his daughter, 'I know you love your Mum, but she can be pretty hard to get along with sometimes.'

'I know,' she sighed.

Paul turned then and bounded up the steps to the house. Vicki could hear him call out as he walked up the hall. 'Been putting on a bit of weight lately, Kate?'

Vicki smiled at the outdoor setting, kicked off her dusty sandals on the bottom step, and followed her parents into the house.

The Removal

'Paddy Ryan isn't well at all,' said Dan, casting an expert eye over the froth on his pint. He took a long draught before continuing, 'Not expected to last the night.'

'Is that right?' said Timmy, distracted, craning his neck to see his reflection in the pub mirror. It was decorated with postcards from customers from such places as Ballybunion and Youghal. Right now, a beach scene from Kilkee was preventing him from checking his James Dean hair do. If they were going to the dance, he wanted to look his best, relaxed and slightly tousled. He had the turn up on the jeans just right, and the check shirt open at the neck. He felt confident, having perfected the brooding smoulder in front of his sister's mirror all afternoon. Judging by the wind howling under the door of Murphy's Bar, he wished he could have got away with bringing his father's old raincoat, only he couldn't, it would have ruined the impression he was aiming for, and probably smelled of dog.

'They'll be there all night, if he goes,' said Dan.

'What?' said Timmy, suddenly aware that Dan's comments were not idle. He hadn't shared the same room as this brother all his life without knowing when Danny was leading up to something.

'But we hardly know Paddy Ryan,' he said, ' and Pa said he's the greatest robber that ever stood behind a shop counter.'

Dan glanced furtively round the bar. 'Be quiet,' he hissed, 'someone will hear you, it's not respectful, and the poor man dying in his bed.'

'I'm only saying,' started Timmy.

'Timmy, my boy,' he said and winked, 'I think it only right that we should pay our respects before it's too late. It's the least that

Pa would have expected us to do.' They both looked down and remained motionless for a moment in memory of their father, who was last seen boarding a train to Dublin, with the gardai close behind.

'But, the dance, Dan. What about the dance?'

'Don't worry, little brother,' he patted Timmy on the head and cried in a loud falsetto, 'Never fear, my dear, Cinderella *shall* go to the ball!' Then he turned to announce, gravely, to the whole bar that he and his brother would now be going to call in on poor old Paddy Ryan, who'd been having a hard time of it lately.

Their fellow drinkers murmured approval, except the landlord, Mick, who snorted his disgust, briskly drying glasses, and muttering to no one in particular, 'Off for free drink, more like. There's never a thought for the livelihood of the publican, I notice, when there's free whiskey to be found at someone's bedside.'

Dan and Timmy made their way to Ryan's and knocked quietly at the door. A neighbour let them in and showed them upstairs to where Paddy was lying in the bed, the curtains drawn and the room oppressively warm. Mary Ryan was sitting by her husband's bedside, gently smoothing his hair back from his forehead. She did not turn round, but continued praying quietly. They stood awkwardly at the foot of the bed, until finally Timmy whispered, 'Hello, Paddy. You're looking grand.' Dan gave him a look that would have killed a horse and moved nearer to the bed, 'Mary, we just came to pay our respects to you all, and to see if there was anything we could do to help.'

'That's very good of you, boys,' she said, straightening her back to look at them. 'Would you ever sit with Paddy for a few minutes while I go down and make some sandwiches. The priest will be here soon to say the rosary.'

'No bother at all, Mary,' said Dan, already regretting the decision to come, and relieved to have something to do that didn't require talking. The two lads sat at either side of the bed trying not to look at Paddy. 'We'd better say a prayer, then,' said Timmy, and as Dan nodded, a terrible sound came from the dying man, like a roar from his throat and then silence.

'What was that?' cried Timmy, almost in tears.

'Jesus, Tim,' said Dan, 'I think he's dead.'

'What are we going to do?' said Timmy jumping up from the chair, 'she'll think we killed him.'

'Don't be such an eejit,' said Dan, 'of course she won't think we killed him. Wasn't he dying anyway? Go and tell her to come up.'

'What? Me?' asked Timmy, 'why do I have to tell her?'

'Would you rather stay here and sit with him?' said Dan.

'Missus,' Timmy said to Mary in the kitchen, 'I think you'd better come. I think...' and he trailed off. Mary dropped a packet of ham on the floor and ran for the stairs.

'Oh, Paddy,' she cried, as she burst into the bedroom. Dan stepped away from the bed so suddenly that he cracked his head on the corner of the dormer window. 'Oh, Paddy,' she cried again, 'you're never gone?' and she threw herself on her husband's body. As she landed on top of him, there was an almighty crack, and both of the Ryans slumped downwards as the metal base broke away from the bed head and crashed to the floor.

'Mother of God,' said Dan, while Timmy stood, mouth open, at the door. Then they rushed to pick up Mary and lift up the end of the bed.

'Oh,' she gasped, 'You'll have to get a lemonade crate from out the back to prop the bed up,' she said to Timmy.

'Better make it two,' Dan cried after him, straining under the weight of the bed and the body. 'He was a fine big man, missus.' he gasped to Mary. 'That he was, Dan,' she said.

When they had secured the bed and rearranged Paddy back on the pillows, Mary sent them downstairs while she stayed at the bedside. The neighbour was buttering bread and they sat quietly in the kitchen. Timmy sneaked a look at his watch. They'd never get to the dance now, and no sign of a drink here when he badly needed one.

Eventually, the undertaker, Mr Skinner arrived with his assistant, and they went into the front room to talk in low voices to the widow. Afterwards they went upstairs and then Mr Skinner came down.

'Look Lads would you ever help us out here,' he said, 'Mrs Ryan would like to have her husband brought down to the front room, and there's only the two of us. We might need a hand. The stairs are very steep and he was a fine big man. We'll get a stretcher from the van, and the four of us should manage OK. We'll need to get him down, the coffin will be coming soon.'

They manoeuvred the stretcher out of the bedroom onto the landing, which was only big enough for two people to pass. They had to hold the stretcher almost vertically in order to turn it to get down the stairs. 'By jiminy, boys, yer man must be eighteen stone.' said Mr Skinner, wheezing hard.

They made a start down the stairs and the weight of the dead man made the stretcher sag in the middle and Paddy Ryan's rear end bounced off every step.

'What's going on?' Mary cried from the kitchen below when she heard the first thump.

'Everything's fine, Mrs Ryan,' said Mr Skinner, 'Timmy here hit his elbow on the wall. Will you try to be more careful there, lad.'

Mary peered up the staircase, into the gloom of a 40-watt light bulb, but was unable to see the stretcher for men crowding around it. Every time her husband's bottom hit a step the undertaker called out, 'Will you try to mind the wall there, boys,' and Dan and Timmy replied in unison, 'Sorry Mr Skinner.' About halfway down the stairs there was another sharp bend. They shuffled the stretcher up to perpendicular, Paddy nearly falling on top of the boys. When Mary saw her husband being hauled down the stairs like a sack of spuds, she ran into the front room, bawling loudly.

Finally, heaving and gasping, they got Paddy into the front room and laid him on the couch. Timmy fell back sweating against the doorjamb, and pushed his sodden hair out of his eyes, all thoughts of James Dean forgotten.

Mary sat at the end of the couch, clutching her rosary beads and staring wide-eyed at her husband. The neighbour came into the room and said, 'Now, boys, I'll get you little drop of something for your trouble,' and the two brothers scrambled out the door after her. They brightened to the clink of bottles but as she fumbled in the press, she said, 'There was never strong liquor allowed in this house,' and they exchanged sour glances to the sound of the soft hiss as she opened a bottle of red lemonade.

FALL FROM GRACE

'THAT COSTUME so becomes you Mademoiselle. Is it for a special occasion?'

Miss Becker pirouetted for her reflection, examining her triptych image in the salon mirrors. She could see no flaw in the way the skirt swept, pencil slim, from waist to just below the knee, a discreet pleat at the back allowing free movement. She walked across the showroom, considering the length of her stride, and the shoes she planned to wear.

'The skirt feels fine, I like the silk of the lining, but I'm not at all sure about the jacket. I think it makes my shoulders look too wide.' She examined herself again in the mirrors, angling her arms forward to assess the 'give' across her back.

'Oh, no Mademoiselle, you look so beautiful,' said the saleswoman, dry brushing her mantis hands. 'And the colour, oh, what light it brings to your eyes.'

Truly the grey-green of the material matched her eyes to perfection. She arched an eyebrow at her reflection. She turned to examine a blue ensemble on the mannequin behind her.

'No,' she murmured, 'the colour is all wrong.' She continued her perusal of the jacket. Single breasted; 100% pure wool, a lining of grey silk; three pearl grey buttons; two faux pockets brushed with a hint of fur, and one small pleat at the rear of the jacket as discreet as its twin on the skirt. So much grey and yet, in the becoming angle of the afternoon light, it looked the colour of a churned green sea.

Miss Becker turned and said swiftly. 'Yes, I'll have it. Send it to the house this afternoon, and find me a blouse, yes, something sheer.'

Ralph will love it, she thought. He always appreciated

whatever she wore; his dark eyes caressing her. When we are married, she thought, and allowed herself the hint of a smile, I will take this costume on my honeymoon. No, better still, I will wear it tomorrow. She emerged on Regent Street, and halted. If my engagement ring is an emerald, it might be too strong a colour in contrast. No, no, it is certain to be a diamond, which will match flawlessly with everything. Ralph had not proposed yet, but he had hinted, oh, how he had hinted. And now he had asked to meet with her urgently.

She hailed a taxi, and directed the driver to her mother's home. They had wedding brochures to examine.

Ralph was waiting for her at the restaurant. The instant he saw the maitre'd escorting her across the room, he leapt to his feet and smiled in welcome.

He helped her out of her jacket, and handed it to the waiter. When they were seated, napkins draped across their laps, he ordered for them both. He spent some moments fussing over the wine list, eventually selecting a modest half bottle of hock.

'So Ralph,' she said, 'your message sounded urgent.'

'Yes, yes,' he said, ' I have something to tell you and didn't want you to hear from someone else.' She sat up straighter at this unexpected overture to his proposal.

'The fact is,' he said, and dabbed his napkin across his glistening forehead, 'the fact is, I have been offered a partnership in a law firm in Boston.'

She allowed her breath to escape slowly. America. Not what she had expected; her mother would be furious, but nevertheless...

'Oh,' she said.

'So, I'm afraid, my dear, that I will be leaving London almost immediately.'

The waiter arrived with the wine, 'I'll pour it myself,' said Ralph waiving him away. They both ignored the bottle in the bucket of ice.

She raised her grey/green eyes from the table and said, 'Oh,' once again.

'I'm so sorry.' he said, 'it's a wonderful opportunity and so unexpected.'

'I thought...' she said but stopped.

'Though what?' he said.

'You led me to believe...' she started, unsure, now, of quite what it was he had led her to believe.

She pushed back her chair, 'You swine,' she said, leaning close to his face. Then she swept away from the table towards the street. Ralph sat, stupefied, staring after her. The waiter caught up to her outside the door, 'Your jacket, Madam,' he said, eyes sparkling with malice. She snatched the jacket out of his hand and flung it into the gutter.

''Ere Stan, did you see that? That woman just flung a coat away.'

'It's just an old coat George,' said Stan, 'what am I looking at it for?'

'It's a beauty, can't you see? Look at that lining.'

'It's dirty,' said Stan

'It could be cleaned though, couldn't it. That coat would be just the job for your Hilda. What do you think?'

'She wouldn't want some stranger's left-overs.'

'Ah, but if you got it cleaned she'd never know the difference. Didn't you say it was her birthday next week? She'll go spare if you don't get her something. And you're as flat brassic as I am,' said George.

'Well, pick it up then and let's get out of here,' said his brother.

His mother found a shirt box of his father's that was white and unmarked, and his sister folded the jacket carefully in tissue paper and placed it gently in the shirt box and wrapped the whole thing in pretty paper. All the buttons were fastened, and the sleeves folded neatly underneath, so that the jacket would smile up, open-faced when Hilda turned back the tissue paper, only the lapels and the designer label showing.

All he needed was a fancy card with flowers and a sloppy verse, she said, and how could any girl resist him?

Stan risked a carnation in his buttonhole when he met Hilda. He had scraped up enough money to take her for a meal, in the café near the station. Hilda was working the evening shift at the telephone exchange, so they met for dinner, or 'lunch' as she kept reminding him to call it. Thoughts of Hilda made him a little dizzy. She was the best looking girl he had ever seen, and he clutched a new white handkerchief, trying to wipe away his nerves and excitement, while he waited for her. When they got into the café and sat down, he shyly pushed the package across the table.

'Happy Birthday, Hil,' he said.

'Oh, Stanley, you are naughty. You shouldn't have. I'll just have the special,' she said to the waitress and Stan nodded that he would have the same. 'And you've bought me a present. Aren't you the sly one?' She put the card on one side, unopened, and tore the wrapping paper off the box. She gave him a delighted, conspiratorial gleam, as she eased the lid open, and slowly pulled back the tissue paper.

'Oh Stan,' she cooed, 'it's beautiful, and the make. My God, you didn't get that down the high street did you?' She pulled the jacket out and held it at arms length, inspecting it.

'Try it on,' said Stan.

'What, here? Ooh I couldn't. Could I?'

'Go on, she won't be back with the dinner for ages yet.'

Hilda looked round the room. She slipped out of her own coat and started opening the jacket buttons. They could see the waitress talking to a couple at another table.

Hilda ran her hand over the rich silk of the lining, and smiled into Stan's anxious face. 'What's this?' she said, looking at something down low down near the hem.

She pulled up the lining to show him small pink piece of paper, held on by a safety pin.

'What? he said, 'what is it?'

'It's a dry cleaning slip,' Hilda's voice had gone flat, 'A bloody, dry cleaning slip. So, that's what you think of me is it? Some old cast off is good enough for me is it? It's a wonder you bothered getting it cleaned. Well I've got news for you, lover boy. You know where you can shove your used goods don't you?' and she threw the jacket across the table, scattering salt and cutlery, and swept out of the cafe.

Stan stood up and looked around helplessly. He grabbed the box and jacket and stumbled outside, and set off over the viaduct towards the pub. Half way across the bridge he caught the box and sent it flying over the railing, followed by the jacket. The white tissue paper floated gently out of sight.

There was a distinctive crack of a button breaking as the jacket hurtled down a bank of scree and litter, coming to stop just yards from a brazier fashioned out of an old tin. A man was hunkered down beside the fire. Near him a woman was rifling through an amalgam of boxes and bags loaded high onto a shopping trolley. They both looked towards the jacket with mild interest.

'Well, well,' she croaked, 'manna from heaven, no less.'

The man grabbed the box and threw it onto the small blaze. 'Waste not, want not,' he chanted, while she bent to pick up the jacket, shaking it hard and brushing off small pebbles and cigarette ends. She gathered up the tissue and folded it carefully and put it in one of the bags on the trolley.

'That's a smashing coat,' he said, 'some of these jokers have got more money than sense.'

The woman did not answer, but shucked off a dirty khaki anorak and slid her bare arms into the cool, velvety sleeves of the jacket.

Making an Impact

'Get on in there, will you.' Da shouted at the cow and gave her a mighty slap on the rump. I watched the hot breath streaming from the cow's mouth and the quiet, reproachful eyes she turned on my father. The look said, don't hurry me, I know the routine as well as you do. This was Lizzie, the oldest cow in the yard and the quietest.

'That's the last,' he cried, to me this time, 'Away you go, and no dawdling and gazing into the heavens. That girl will still be there when the cows are milked.' I coloured at this and made no reply, just went to the corner of the shed to get my stool and bucket. The gleaming churns were lined up ready to go on the cart, and I needed to get a move on if I was to get all six cows milked and me ready in time for Mass.

I'll do Hetty first today, I thought, and looked around quickly afraid that I had spoken out loud. Da would scoff at me if he knew I gave the cows names, but he was gone out of the shed, and I could hear the flup of his rubber boots hitting the back of his legs as he trudged off to the house for his first cup of tea of the day. My mother would be in there making porridge, only a small fire made, enough for the breakfast. She'd save me the porridge and brew fresh tea when I got back. I rubbed my hands together vigorously to try to bring some warmth into them. He'd mock me too if he knew I warmed my hands for the cows. The first milking of the day was always a torment to me. I was no natural early riser and vowed every day to myself that my brother could have the farm; he'd get no argument from me. I'd be off to Cork as soon as I could and make my mark in the world there, not be buried here in the dark hills scratching a living like my father and his father before him out of land that broke your heart and your back. But Jimmy looked like he had beaten me to it, studying engineering in Dublin, and the parents giving me sidelong looks and wondering between themselves what will become of the farm. Well, they weren't going to blackmail me into a life getting up at four o'clock every morning, even if their hopes rested on me. Life on the farm was hard, the weather unforgiving and the few acres yielding barely enough to keep body and soul together. I squared my shoulders to the frosty dawn, pulled up the stool to Hetty, gave her a pat, and set about milking.

As soon as my father's footsteps had faded away the black cat sloped into the shed followed by her last surviving kitten. She was the scrawniest cat you ever saw, old now and tired from all the kittens she'd had over the years. Before she fetched up at this place she must have got caught in a rabbit trap. Her right front paw was gone completely and a piece of grey bone stuck out of what remained of her leg. It didn't slow her up much though, and she was up to every trick. Now she was teaching the kitten the best way to get a drink of milk. She sat quietly with the kitten beside her, watching me, and when I moved the teat to point in their direction they both leapt onto their back feet and reached up, mouths wide open, to catch the stream of warm milk I aimed at them. She came every morning and I had lost count of the generations of kittens she had trained to do this before she hunted them completely to make way for a new litter. When I was a boy I used to smuggle scraps of meat out of the house for her, not that there was ever much to spare, but I didn't hold with that kind of nonsense now. The cat had to fend for herself like the rest of us, not like the poor old cows that had helplessness bred into them.

As I settled into the rhythm of milking, my head leaning on Hetty's warm flank, I started daydreaming again about the day to come.

I'd have to do something about the bike. Jimmy and myself had fixed it up, to be fit to ride, out of the scraps and parts of a couple of other old bikes we found abandoned in the barn, and some begged and borrowed bits from friends and neighbours. A tattered old homemade bike wasn't exactly the sophisticated image I had in mind. I'd have liked to have driven up in a new car rather than turning up on a bike that required strenuous pressure on the front mudguard to assist the brakes, which often seized up at crucial moments. I had my good suit that I always wore to Mass. Jimmy had brought it back for me from Dublin on one of his visits, as strange himself with his city talk and affectations as any foreigner we had ever met, which admittedly were few. He would look out the kitchen window, leaning casually on the sill, one hand in his pocket, whistling softly to himself. If he caught me watching him he would shake his head sadly and give me that pitying 'rather you than me' look. The suit was a salve to his conscience, but it was a fine one all the same and made me feel quite the swell with my white shirt, blue tie and shoes so clean you could see your face in them.

Maryanne had agreed to meet me after Mass today at the bottom of town by the park. If I closed my eyes I could see her running down the hill, chestnut hair streaming out behind her, and her laughter echoing all the way up the rise. The thought of her made me smile. I had walked out for a short while the previous year with a girl from the next village, but I had never visited her home, nor she mine. She was a non-stop talker, enough to give a fellow a headache, as was her mother, and her father was known to be the meanest man for five miles. A quieter girl would suit me better, I was thinking.

When the milking was done and the cows led back out to the field, I headed to the house, frowning as I went at the dark clouds gathering overhead, and at the mist bearing down heavily on the mountains. There would be time enough for rain after I had met Maryanne at the park, and I said a silent prayer that it would hold off for the afternoon. Sunday was the only chance I had to go into the village and while away a few hours. We had known each other all our lives, Maryanne and I, growing up on adjoining farms, and going to school together. But I suddenly saw her last week as if she were a stranger, and she made me feel shy and awkward. I couldn't get over how that scrawny little kid with a carroty head and braces on her teeth had turned into this beauty without my noticing. She was the youngest of four sisters and all the others had married and moved away. I suppose, I thought dryly, her parents are giving her sidelong looks as well. These days a girl was not so looked down on in the farming business, and as they had no boy to carry on the farm, Maryanne carried the burden of family hopes, but she seemed to do it in a more light hearted way than I was managing.

The dog, Tigger, raced up delighted and followed me to the tap at the back of the house. He always knew when a trip to town was in the offing. He watched carefully as I washed my head and hands under the tap, a new fangled contraption that would have horrified my grandfather when he lived here, but we took to with gratitude for saving us a half-mile walk to the well and back every day.

'No trip for you, today, my boy,' I said to Tigger, 'I'm taking the bike. I have a young lady to meet, and I'm not turning up in a dirty old cart and risk you jumping mud over her good dress.'

My mother had breakfast ready in the kitchen, an egg today and freshly made brown bread to go with the porridge, and she had water boiling for my shave. She knew I was meeting someone, but didn't tease me like the Da did, just ironed me a clean shirt, and left me to myself.

I had no bicycle clips so I had to make a fold in my trouser legs and tuck them inside my socks for fear of them being caught in the chain. This rather spoiled the effect of the suit, but better than arriving covered in grease.

I fidgeted through the service, and dodged Mrs Brown from down the road who would have all my business out of me before I knew what I was saying. At last I jumped on the bike and set off for the park. The weather was holding, and I wanted to get there before Maryanne so that I could practice leaning on the railing, casually, the way Jimmy had stood at the window. I wondered if I should smoke, but too late to bother with that now. The suit would have to do the business as far as style went.

I hit the hill at a fair clip, and sped down past the pub and the post office and the shops. As I got near the bottom of the hill, I wished I had a watch. I was getting anxious. Suppose she got there before me, would she decide I wasn't coming or would she wait?

And there she was, standing quite still looking towards the park. I breathed a sigh of relief and hit the brakes. There was a grating sound, but no slowing down. I put my foot on the front mudguard with great force and the old bike screeched a protest though a blur of burning rubber. I flew over the handlebars and landed at Maryanne's feet, the bike on top of me. Without a word she lifted the bike off me and stepped back so I could get up by myself, and maintain some shred of dignity. I didn't dare look at her to see the spark of laughter in her eyes that I knew would be there. The suit was in shreds, both knees gaping and a large tear at the shoulder. I was bleeding freely from both legs and had twisted my ankle.

'We'd better get that gash washed up,' she said, when it was clear that my injuries were more to my pride than anything else. 'Will we go up to the house?' I nodded yes. She pushed my bike even though I protested, and the front wheel was so badly buckled that she was half carrying it. We hardly spoke as we laboured back up the hill. I was too mortified to speak and Maryanne kept her own counsel.

As we reached the crest of the hill the sun suddenly spread over the sky. We both stopped, my knee was getting painful now, but the sight between the trees was beautiful and I sighed happily.

When we arrived at the door, Maryanne leaned the bike carefully against the hedge. Then she looked at me and we both smiled a little.

'Will you come in?' I asked.

'I will,' she said, and I led her into the house.

Cherry Tree Inn

'Long before your great, great grandfather came to Grenfell, about the middle of the nineteenth century, the Wiradjuri tribe roamed all over this land from up near Bathurst. Bathurst is the first inland city in Australia, bet you didn't know that. They travelled all the way down to the Victorian border. Of course, it was called Emu Creek then.'

'Why did they change the name then, Dad?' asked Alice. She knew the story as well as he did, but loved to hear him tell it. Rare was the day she got to spend with her father. He worked odd shifts for the railway, but the two of them would ride into town on their bikes, when he had the time, and get supplies, 'to save your mother,' as he said. 'She needs her rest.' He never said why her mother needed rest when she had always seemed so lively before, cleaning and cooking from morning till night, but lately, even Alice had been asked to do little chores around the house to help her mother, 'so that she could rest.'

' That,' he said, 'would be after the commissioner's stagecoach was held up and he was killed by bushrangers, way back. I've told you about the gold, haven't I? See those hills, gold everywhere there was, all gone now mind.' He chuckled to himself, 'Imagine, old man Wood was here for over thirty years and never knew the place was seamed with gold till his shepherd, O'Brien, spotted it. His sheep shearing days were well and truly over when the nuggets started to surface.'

They stopped outside the post office and leaned their bikes against the wall. Alice raced to get to the drapers where they had for sale the most beautiful ribbons she had ever seen. She had sixpence in the tiny purse clutched in her hand. Having money of any kind was almost unheard of, and being able to spend it on anything she liked was probably the most exciting thing that had happened to her, ever. As she was ten years old she was quite big enough, her mother had told her this morning, to choose her own ribbon to decorate her hat for church tomorrow. It took her long, agonising minutes to choose the right ribbon. She hopped from one foot to the other as the draper wrapped the tiny bundle of eighteen cerise inches of ribbon in brown paper and tied a loop in the string of her parcel so that she could hang it on the handlebars of her bike. She rolled the word, cerise, around her tongue and clutched the brown paper bundle to her breast, afraid she would burst with joy, as she ran out of the shop to find her father.

Panniers overflowing, they set back along the track, her father telling her all his stories from the old days and quoting from Henry Lawson's poems. His loud, strong voice and shouts of laughter bounced back at them from the valleys of Weddin Mountains. He had taught her the names of the wildflowers and ferns and shown her where to find water. He told her that the Wiradjuri had taught him all their bush craft, but he smiled and winked when he said it, so that she knew he was pulling her leg. There were not many tribesmen around these days.

Now, in late October, the spring flowers were beginning to bloom, and he promised her a trip soon to see the bush orchids and stringy bark trees, and to scratch her name on one of the sandstone cliffs that loomed over the valleys.

'Not next week, mind,' he said as they rode home, 'and maybe not the week after. It all depends on your mother.' He smiled down at her, peddling slowly, so that she could keep up. Then he cleared his throat. 'How would you like someone to play with? Someone of your very own to care for and to love?' She looked up at him, nervous and excited and shy all at once. 'Love' wasn't a word much used in the bush. And if he meant that her cousin Albert was coming to visit again from Bathurst, she could well do without him, he was a bully and a brute. The only pleasure she got out of his last visit was when he was thrashed for putting a red-back spider in her doll's pram.

'What do you mean, Dad?' she asked, and he cleared his throat again and said. 'We'll have to ask your mother. Come over this way and I'll show you the ruins of the Cherry Tree Hotel.' As their tyres made patterns in the dust around the old derelict pub, her father recited from Lawson's poem:

The rafters are open to sun, moon, and star,
Thistles and nettles grow high in the bar --
The chimneys are crumbling; the log fires are dead,
And green mosses spring from the hearthstone instead.
The voices are silent, the bustle and din,
For the railroad hath ruined the Cherry-tree Inn.

'Just as well, eh, Alice, or your poor old dad wouldn't have a job with the railways?'

As they approached their house, they could see that Uncle Jim and Auntie Nola were there, their small truck pulled up outside the gate. Uncle Jim looked gravely down at Alice when he saw her, and made her turn around while he examined her from head to foot, and peered closely at her hands, 'I need to see how clean you keep them, girlie. No grubby hands or bitten nails for the job I have for you.' She glanced nervously at her mother, but could see that all the adults were smiling at her.

'Now Alice,' said Uncle Jim, 'I've been talking to your mother and we think you're big enough now to take on a very responsible job. What do you think?'

'Oh, yes, Uncle Jim,' she said, 'I'm ten now and make my own bed and dry the dishes.'

'In that case I think you're old enough for the job I have for you.' The whole family went out to the small shed in the backyard. Even before they got there, Alice could hear a feeble bleating coming from inside, and huddled in the corner on a bed of old newspapers and straw, was a tiny lamb, no more than a month old Uncle Jim told her, and abandoned by the mother who had had triplets. 'This one has been hand reared.' Her uncle explained, but now needed to be looked after for a bit longer. 'Do you think you're up to the job?'

'Oh, yes,' breathed Alice. This must have been what Dad meant by someone of her own to look after and love. 'I'll call her Hermione,' she said, and her parents laughed and said that was a fine name for an orphaned lamb.

Although Alice's hints about putting a bed down for the lamb in her own room were ignored, she spent every moment she could feeding Hermione and playing with her and was allowed to take out an old blanket to put on the straw on the shed floor.

On Friday when she came home from school, her mother was missing, and Auntie Nola was making tea in the kitchen. 'Your Dad and Mum have had to go into town. Uncle Jim lent them the truck. I'll be here with you for a couple of days.'

'What's the matter,' cried Alice. Her mother was always there when she got home from school. Now the house smelled different, everything looked different, her aunt had her hat on the hook behind the door where her mother's hat was always hanging, and she was frightened. 'Where have they gone? Is my dad sick? Is something wrong with Mum?'

'No. No,' said Auntie Nola, laughing, 'nothing like that at all. Your mum just has to go into town for a couple of days. There's nothing at all to worry about. When they come back, they'll be bringing you a wonderful surprise. And in the meantime, you and I will have lots of fun together, won't we? I'm cooking a lamb chop for your tea.'

'A lamb chop!' cried Alice. 'I'm not eating a lamb chop. I'm not eating Hermione. I want my Mum.'

'Now stop being a silly girl,' said her auntie, 'change your clothes and wash your hands and you can set the table for me. Uncle Jim will be coming over soon for his tea and he won't want to see tears and tantrums, now will he? I'll get you a nice boiled egg instead of the lamb chop. How does that sound? Your mum and dad will be back in no time.'

Alice ran out to the shed and wept as she hugged Hermione tightly to her. Hermione was her only friend. Everything had changed and Alice was frightened and unhappy. She finally went into the house. She pushed her egg and toast around the plate, and wouldn't even drink the sweet tea that Auntie Nola gave her.

The next day, her parents were still not back. Auntie Nola made comforting noises, and went about the business of cleaning the house and making the meals. Uncle Jim had gone back to his farm to look after his sheep and Alice stayed most of the day with Hermione, and hugged her and told her how miserable she was, and she wanted her mum and dad back, and things to be the way they were. 'I don't want to live with Auntie Nola,' she whispered,' and pressed her unhappy face into the lamb's neck. Just then her aunt called her to come in and lay the table for lunch, and she slouched into the house, even forgetting to leave her shoes outside on the back verandah.

The afternoon dragged on. Her parents had gone away and her lamb wouldn't play with her. Was it because she hadn't made her bed this morning and was rude to Auntie Nola when she made her some cocoa last night? 'I don't want cocoa. It's too hot for cocoa. I want my mum. Don't you know anything?'

'Now, now, girlie,' said Uncle Jim quietly, 'that's no way to speak to your auntie; she's only trying to look after you till your mum comes back. You wouldn't want you mum and dad to hear you being rude like that, now, would you?' And she fled to her own little room, and slammed the door and threw herself on the bed sobbing.

On Sunday morning she woke early, while the house was still quiet, and decided that she wasn't going to go to church or school or anything until her parents came back. She would take a blanket and a packet of biscuits and stay in the shed with Hermione. By the time she slipped out of the house, she could hear her auntie moving about in the kitchen preparing breakfast. Alice slipped quietly out the back door and headed for the shed.

Uncle Jim's truck came slowly round the corner and pulled up outside the gate. Alice's father jumped out and ran round to open the door for his wife and their precious new bundle, and led them gently towards the front door. As they entered the house, they hear a wail from the backyard, and Alice burst into the kitchen, 'Hermione's not moving, Hermione's dead.' she cried and threw herself into her father's arms.

'Now, now, Alice,' said her Dad, 'come and see what your mum has for you, a beautiful new baby sister.' He started to lead her over towards the baby, 'Come and see Barbara, and say hello.'

Through a blur of tears Alice stared horrified at the bundle in her mother's arms. 'What sister,' she cried, 'I don't want a sister. I want Hermione. Take her away; take her back where she came from. I hate her. I hate her!' And, howling in anguish and rage, she threw open the fly screen door and ran and ran.

Nothing

'What's so funny?'

'Humm?'

'What's so funny?'

He lowered the newspaper and looked at her over his glasses. 'What do you mean?'

'You just laughed, and I asked you what was so funny,' she replied.

'Oh, nothing,' he said, and shook the paper to straighten it again.

'Nothing that would interest me, you mean.'

'That's right, Ruth, nothing that would interest you.'

'And when did you become the expert on what would interest me, then?'

He lowered the paper again, then slowly and neatly folded it, front page upwards, and laid it carefully on the table.

'What's the matter now, Ruth?'

'Apart from you treating me like an idiot you mean.'

'For the love of God, Ruth, what's got into you?'

'Nothing,' she snapped and stabbed her knife into the marmalade.

'Have I forgotten your birthday or something?' he said.

'Don't be ridiculous. You know full well my birthday was last month. I just wanted to know what you were laughing at in the paper. Is that so wrong?'

He observed the sunlight dancing on dust motes as they drifted towards the table. Then he said in a small voice, from far a way, 'it was a cartoon about the government and the economy. I'll show it to you, if you like.'

'No, thank you, very much. I'm sick to death of the government and the economy, as you well know.'

Deprivation

'We'll go over the rules one more time, so there's no mistake.'

The Governor stood stiffly to attention as Reynolds, the chief warder, started to read to the prisoner from the clipboard.

'Three months in solitary confinement, monitored for variations to blood pressure and heart beat,' he gestured with his head towards the instruments that the prisoner was to use for this purpose. They had gone over the routine a number of times, so that there would be no need to open the reinforced door once the experiment had started. Biggs had joked he could get a job as a nurse when he got out, all the training he had done.

Reynolds cleared his throat and went on, 'Diary entries of mood,' here he rolled his eyes and Biggs smiled broadly at him, 'diet, sensory and physical matters of interest,' he continued.

'What physical matters would you find of interest, eh, Mr Reynolds?' asked Biggs, maintaining the broad grin. Reynolds scowled and gave a quick glance towards the Governor, who looked straight ahead and ignored the exchange.

'As I was saying, matters of interest to the medicos as per the questionnaires provided for each day. Notations to be made each morning on awakening. These completed questionnaires are to be slid through the opening provided in the door.' The two men looked towards the reinforced steel door. There was no door handle visible, just a list of the rules pasted to the back, above a narrow horizontal slit just wide enough to feed a single piece of A4 paper through. The Governor maintained his gaze, giving no indication of hearing Reynolds' nasal drone.

'The time that the prisoner wakes will be presumed to be the morning for the purposes of this exercise, so a form is to be filled up each time you wake. Right?' he asked.

'Right,' said the prisoner.

The warder turned a page on his clipboard. 'Successful completion of this experiment will result in early parole for the prisoner, Leonard Biggs, effective one week after the last day of this incarceration.'

'Right,' said Biggs, rubbing his hands together.

'Mutual examination and agreement of facilities and conditions to commence,' barked Reynolds.

Biggs looked round the small room with interest, as this was the first time he had seen it. Their practice runs had always been performed in the small room adjoining the Governor's office. Although the experiment was supposed to be very hush hush to avoid complaints from the other prisoners of preferential treatment for Biggs, the news had spread quickly through the prison. 'Jammy bugger,' said his cellmate Blacko, but some of the others said they wouldn't risk their sanity in that black hole for *ten* years off, let alone three. But Biggs scoffed. He was in a hurry to leave, and he couldn't wait to get one over on the hated Reynolds.

'Back again, Lenny? Fancy that, and you such a genius and all,' the warder would say and roar with laughter. 'Don't tell me that missus of yours is still hanging around waiting for a no hoper like you. I just might have to go round and see how she's getting on.'

It was a pleasant enough room, with cream walls, no windows, of course, but bright fluorescent lights which could not be turned off from within the room. There was a single divan bed, with a wooden headboard; a bedside table with a diary already in place and a box of felt tipped pens. In the middle of the room was a table and two chairs. Two chairs, he smiled to himself, who do they think I'm going to be entertaining? There was also a burgundy leather armchair, very comfortable looking, with a reclining mechanism. All the furniture was fixed to the floor. They did not want the subject to start wreaking his frustration on the furniture, and they were in no doubt that frustration would come, even for a reasonably placid and unimaginative man like Biggs. There was no television, no radio, no computer, tapes, cds, playing cards or any other means of entertainment. Lenny was not a reader, so he was not dismayed at the lack of distractions. The noise in the prison was continuous, whether it was day or night and he was looking forward to some time to think, to lie back in the recliner with a coffee in one hand and a cigarette in the other, planning his future and the next job that he knew would be his passport to easy living.

On the wall about a metre above the door was a camera trained on the room, another on each of the other walls at the same height. The entire room could be scanned from the control room every three minutes, and each quarter of the room would be constantly on screen for CCTV observation. A warder and a psychologist would be monitoring Lenny's movements at all times, day and night, whether he would know when it was day or night. He had been warned that he would most likely become disoriented and lose a proper sense of time, but he silently scoffed at this idea. Just get on with it, he thought, the sooner it's over, the sooner I'm gone from this miserable pile of bricks.

On the smooth metal door, above the list of rules was a large red button with a sign over it, also in red, which declared, in capital letters, 'Not to be used except in extreme emergency. Evacuation of the test area prior to completion of experiment will rescind any prior agreement.'

'That means, Biggs, when you're in, you're in, and no good complaining you've forgotten your toothbrush.' Reynolds laughed at his own joke but was ignored by both the prisoner and the Governor.

'All facilities are provided, he continued, 'everything you need. Food is either dried, tinned or frozen. Your *culinary* preferences have been taken into account. Sounds like the condemned man's last meal doesn't it?' he laughed. The Governor finally turned his gaze towards him, and Reynolds straightened his tie and rushed on, 'there is an electric kettle for coffee and tea; a microwave for cooking and heating up food. Room heating is of the under floor variety and ventilation is provided by a concealed air conditioning unit. No alcohol is allowed but the Governor,' here he hesitated and shot a disapproving glance in the direction of his boss, who had resumed his steady gaze at the opposite wall, 'the Governor, in the interests of your *comfort*, has agreed to your request for tobacco. The air conditioning is designed to cope with any air pollutants, but there is also an extractor fan above the bed if the nicotine haze gets too much.'

Warder and prisoner exchanged malevolent looks. Permission for the prisoner had been hard won, the warder disagreeing vigorously with such a concession. 'All the comforts of home', he argued, were hardly conducive to creating the conditions of deprivation required for an experiment. But the psychologist in charge had decided that the physical and mental effects of such a long period of isolation could be adequately monitored without depriving the subject of his cigarettes. It was considered that the nicotine withdrawal symptoms resulting in a refusal of tobacco would skew the results of the research. Biggs had also convinced the Governor that he enjoyed a cigarette now and again but was in no way dependent on them. Reynolds knew, of course, that almost all the inmates were chain smokers and that Biggs was no exception.

Biggs gave a cursory glance at the appliances and fridge, but carefully examined the contents of the cupboards. He wouldn't put it past Reynolds to 'accidentally' forget to put the cigarettes there for him, but sure enough there were enough cartons of his brand to keep him going for a lot longer than he needed. He breathed deeply, imagining the sweetness of the smoke being drawn into his lungs. No more scrounging roll your owns from now on. 'Yeah,' he said, 'looks OK.' Easy, he thought, three months holed up here in the lap of luxury and I'm home free with three years wiped off the slate.

'You are also provided with an exercise machine.' Reynolds nodded towards the equipment, and shook his head at the folly. Biggs flexed his shoulder muscles. Got to keep in shape. He had already spent most of the last month in the gym.

'The ablution area is behind that screen, en suite, you might say, but remember you will be under surveillance the whole time.' That's all right, boyo, thought Biggs, you have your fun. I'll give you a big wave when I skip out the front gate.

'Your bedding and clothing you will have to wash yourself. Machine and dryer provided, as you can see. All the lights remain on all the time, as you know. There is a back up generator in case of failure of the mains. If you can't sleep with the light on, you can always put a pillow over your head.' Again, a small movement by the Governor wiped the smirk off his face, and he turned to the last page on his clipboard. 'If you become ill or distressed the experiment will cease and your parole agreement will be cancelled. Agreed?'

'Agreed,' said the prisoner, and stepped forward to sign the document.

'Well, um, Leonard,' the Governor spoke for the first time, 'that seems to be about all. Best of luck to you, and we'll see you in thirteen weeks.'

'Yes, sir,' said Biggs, and the Governor quickly left the room.

Reynolds had a quick look round, tucked the clipboard under his arm and smirked at Biggs. 'Have a nice time, *Leonard,*' made a mock salute and left.

Lenny made a dismissive gesture at the closing door, gave a quick glance at the surveillance camera and danced around the room briefly, shadow boxing and admiring himself in the mirror.

He pulled out a chair and sat at the table, whistling quietly, hands in his pockets as he looked around the room. Then he went and sat on the side of the bed and bounced a little. Nice, he thought, better than the rubbish in the cells. He decided to make a cup of coffee and was just about to pick up the kettle when he noticed something. He looked along the bench top by the sink, in the drawers, in the cupboard under the sink. He opened the store cupboard, felt under the mattress, under the pillow. He opened the fridge and the microwave, checked under the table, down the side of the armchair. He pulled everything out of the cupboards and piled it in the middle of the floor. He rubbed his hands through his hair and then took a kick at one of the cigarette cartons and sent it flying, cracking the box open and sending packets of cigarettes slamming into the wall. 'No lighter, no matches' he croaked, and threw himself face down on the bed.

The Houseboat

SCARGILL LIVED on a houseboat with his wife, Patti. I did not know that when I first saw him, in the pub, trying to put his hand up the barmaid's skirt.

'Keep your filthy hands to yourself, slime ball,' she hissed, as she leaned over to collect glasses from his table. She was well able to handle him, and gave his roving hand a sharp slap. He must have been used to this response, since his features did not change from a lascivious leer.

He was an unfortunate looking fellow with a large head and murky grey, protruding eyes. He looked like a candidate for and over active thyroid, which would have accounted for the eyes, but the only thing over active about Scargill seemed to be his imagination if he thought he could make a play for the barmaid. I could see that he was steadily working his way through numerous pints followed by whiskey chasers, and looked settled in for the afternoon with a couple of back slapping pals. He lumbered to his feet to play darts and when he raised his arm to aim at the board, his shirt pulled out of his trousers and his gelatinous bulk shook, seemingly unconnected to any skeletal structure.

He was about my age, mid fifties, but I keep myself fit. I had recently accepted a redundancy, and was considering what direction my life would take next. In the meantime I decided to take a month off and relax, get the kinks out of my shoulders after years hunched over various ledgers. I booked a small chalet by the river and set out my running gear and golf clubs along with the laptop on which I intended to write either an expose of corporate greed or a detective thriller, both genres I was forced to admit having been done to death of late.

I like things tidy, orderly. I am not tall for a man and suffered many slights because of it, but I knew I could handle myself if need be. I did weights and aerobic exercises every day, and ran five miles, five days a week.

After a few days settling in I had established a routine that suited me. I rose early, had a light breakfast and went for my run. I had measured the route. If I went along the road near my chalet, up a side lane, avoided the main street and doubled back past the church, I could take a breather on the bench beside the river, and that was exactly two and a half miles. I bought the paper, drank some water, and relaxed under the shade of a sultry willow, before setting off for the second leg of my constitutional. In the afternoon I wandered into town for provisions and sometimes dropped by the Horse and Hounds for a quick half, before going home to cook a stir-fry or prepare a salad. It did not bother me, having no one to talk to and I made no effort to engage in conversation with anyone in the shop or the pub. I was happy to observe, and speculated that Scargill, would make a good study for the villain in my, as yet, unstarted novel.

The houseboat was moored close to where I sat at the half way mark of my run, a shabby husk of a craft, faded paint showed her name to be 'Trail Blazer'; not the kind of name you would automatically associate with the blubbery lecher I'd seen at the pub.

One day I was late with my run and arrived at the bench in the early afternoon. As I sat there, sipping water and scanning the sports pages, I heard crashing and saw Scargill trudging down the short gangplank onto the jetty from the boat. He dragged himself slowly up the steps leading to the road. He passed so close by me I could hear his laboured breathing, but he gave no sign that he had seen me, and I retreated behind my paper. I had no wish to engage in conversation with such a sluggard. I sat idly for a while watching the light play on the water, enjoying the peace. Just then a woman, short and slight with dark hair, appeared on the deck of the houseboat. She sat in a deck chair and pulled out needles and wool and started knitting. I gradually realised that she was also checking me out. I was embarrassed that she might think I was some sort of a pervert and I left hurriedly.

This encounter worried me, though. I value my good name and it rankled that this woman might think badly of me. Also, to be honest, I thought with Scargill for a husband, she had enough to worry about without checking for prowlers. A couple of days later, I took my run after lunch again, and, sure enough, up he plodded on his way to the pub. Like me, he had a routine, but his was to hit the pub early afternoon, have a skinful and then lurch home through the twilight to sleep it off.

She soon appeared, but this time she came ashore with a small dog, so I stepped forward and said, 'I hope I didn't startle you the other day. I was just having a breather and admiring the river.'

She was a little flustered and very shy, so I admired the dog and remarked on the weather and such, and she relaxed a bit. I continued my run then and she walked off with the dog. I often saw her after that, and we had a bit of a chat. We usually stood by the bench, under the willow tree, had a few words, and went on our way. I thought nothing of this. I had no evil intent, no designs on her. I had so far successfully managed to remain a bachelor despite some determined assaults on my single status when I was younger. And anyway, she was a married woman.

One afternoon when it was very hot, I stooped over near the bench, feet splayed, hands on my knees, panting a bit. I had forgotten my water bottle and it was a lot hotter that day than I had realised. Patti, as I had come to know her, must have noticed me and came up the steps to ask me if I wanted a drink. 'Yes, please,' I said, and followed her down to the boat. I assumed I would wait while she went aboard and fetched a glass of lemonade or something, but she said, 'Come on, you can sit on the deck,' so I did. Her knitting bag was there and about a dozen different coloured knitted squares. She had told me that the Women's Institute met every week, making blankets for Ethiopian orphans. This seemed to be the only time she got out. That slob of a husband never took her anywhere, and she never mentioned any family. She disappeared below and I leaned back in the deckchair and closed my eyes, soaking up the sunshine.

I was startled out of my reverie when the boat keeled dangerously to one side, and a huge shadow in front of me blotted out the sun.

'What the bloody hell d'you think you're doing on my boat with my missus,' he roared, prodding my chest with a big, beefy finger. I started to stammer some sort of explanation, trying to rise out of the low chair when Patti appeared on deck, smiling and carrying two glasses on a tray.

Scargill howled when he saw her, and, forgetting about me, and moving faster than I would have thought possible, lurched towards her with his fist raised. Before I could recover my wits, he tripped over the knitting bag, caught his foot up in a skein of wool and stumbled forward. I grabbed the nearest thing, which was the knitting bag, and swung it at his head, just to put him off course, but he lumbered sideways and disappeared headlong over the side of the boat. There was a sickening thud, followed by a soft sigh as the water parted to receive him. Patti and I were frozen to the spot, staring at each other for long seconds and then we rushed to look over the rail, but there was no sign of him. We scanned the shallows. I leaned far out over the bow but all I could see was churned up silt and some sort of molluscs clinging to the boat. I contemplated diving in after him, but I am not a strong swimmer, and I recoiled at the prospect of grappling all that soft, slippery flesh.

'I'll get help,' I said, and Patti just stared into the water.

The police came, the lifeguard and the ambulance, and eventually they found him, his bloated hulk snagged on the propeller of 'Trail Blazer'.

There seemed no point in complicating the affair, so I told the sergeant that I was on the riverside, sitting on the bench under the willow tree when I saw him fall. Patti gave me a quick, startled look, but said nothing.

The pathologist reported later that Scargill had struck his head on the bank when he fell, and unconscious, sank beneath the boat, which was why we couldn't see him. The report also said that his alcohol level was three times over the limit, so, essentially, it was the beer and the blow to the head that did for him.

A woman from the Women's Institute came and took Patti home with her for a few days, and I offered to mind the dog, he was a nice little chap. As her friend was leading her away, I impulsively reached over and squeezed her hand and mumbled my condolences. She had not cried or even spoken, except to tell the detective that her husband had become entangled in the knitting, which he could see was still strewn across the deck. The doctor thought she was in shock and prescribed a sedative. When I touched her hand, she gave a little start, and then, looking up, smiled weakly at me.

She gave me a key for the cabin where the dog food was kept. I trotted him back to my place and he settled in quickly, sitting in the middle of the kitchen watching me with his mouth open and tongue lolling, the way dogs look like they are smiling. I cut up some cooked chicken for him; that dog food on the boat did not look very appetising, and he golloped the meat quick smart.

I enjoyed taking him with me jogging, and each day we went back to the boat to make sure everything was all right, ship shape, you might say.

Patti was due back by the weekend so I stocked up the fridge. It was so quiet on the river; all you could hear was the gentle lapping of the water just below the gunnels. I looked around the orderly galley kitchen, and tidy living area; she kept the small place neat and inviting. Obviously I did not open the door at the end which must lead to the bedroom Patti shared with... I did not like to think of her sharing anything with him, let alone a bed. I felt a small shiver of disgust, but shook it off.

I made a cup of tea and sat on the deck, the dog smiling up at me. I could see along the length of the river, a glittering, undulating path, inviting me forward. A feeling of peace came over me, as if my bones had just now settled into the right configuration, the right space.

'What do you think, old fellow?' I asked the dog, who wagged his tail agreeably at me, 'I wouldn't take up as much room as him would I?'

Family Ties

I'm standing on the step, looking at the peeling paint on the doorframe and the smeared glass, cracked down the middle. There's no doorbell or knocker so I rap a few times on the glass. I know she would have seen me walking down the road, but she'll make me wait on the step, just because she can. After a minute or two, I rap again, louder and harder this time, and hear her yelling from the back of the house, 'Alright, no need to knock the blasted door down.' Two more minutes, I time it, and she opens the door as far as the security chain would let her. Who in their right mind would bother putting a security chain on a broken glass door? 'Oh, it's you,' she says. 'Who the hell else would it be?' I ask. She doesn't bother to answer me but turns and yells up the stairs, 'Joe, your dad's here. Shut that Nintendo off.' Then she turns to me again, bleary eyes peering at me through a tatty looking fringe. About time she got her roots done. 'He needs shoes,' she says. I know he needs shoes, and she knows I lost my job. 'I don't have money for shoes,' I say. 'You're behind with your payments,' she says, blowing cigarette smoke out the door into my face, just because she knows I'd given up. I look away, at the bloke next door, changing the oil on his motorbike, spilling it all over the place, oil running down the gutter where two little girls are playing at the edge of the kerb. That'll shift them. I can hear Joe clattering down the stairs. He'll start to bellyache in a minute, same thing every week. 'I don't want to go with him,' he says, in what's supposed to be a whisper, but sounds like an earthquake to me. 'Get your shoes on,' his mother says, ignoring him, and then to me, 'have him back for six, and no sweets or he won't eat his supper.'

She undoes the chain and Joe junior slouches out without looking at me. 'Hello, Joe,' I say, and grab his hand, 'let's go to the park for a while.' He doesn't bother to answer. Why should he? We do the same thing every week, he plays on the swings and throws sand around in the sandpit, while I read the paper, and then I take him home. Can't afford anything else, at least it's not raining. A couple of hours, and I've done my fatherly duty.

I settle myself on the bench and read bits of the paper. Just finished the sports page and having a look at the comics and look up to check on Joe. He's okay, playing in the sandpit, with a weedy looking kid next to him digging holes with a pink plastic shovel. His parents are sitting on the bench, Mr and Mrs Cashmere, in their smart casual clothes. He's sitting there with the Sunday Times, no less, and she's reading some book or other, and looking up now and then to admire her pride and joy in the sandpit.

I'm reading the paper, minding my own business when I hear this high prissy voice saying, 'No, no, little boy. Don't throw the sand about. Little boys must play nicely.' Oh, boy. Her highness is having a go at my Joe. Just to show her what I think of her and her whiny, plummy voice, I spit onto the concrete path. I can see her out of the corner of my eye looking disgusted. So I say to Joe, 'You go right ahead. This here's a public sandbox.'

So then, the bloke realises something's going on, and lowers his paper slowly onto his designer jeans, looks over his glasses and turns his weaselly little eyes over to me, and smiles as if he's done something wrong. 'Oh,' he says, ' that's right, of course, but children need to play safely.'

I'm sick of being pushed around by the likes of him, so I say, 'My kid's got as much right to be here as yours and if you don't like it you can take your kid and get the hell out of here.' So then this clown makes to get up, draws himself up to his full 5'6". 'Now look here,' he says. This scrawny white-faced clown, with his cross trainers and his gold watch. Looks like he hasn't had a decent meal in a month. I'm looking at his hand holding the paper. He's so thin, his fingers look like hair growing on bones.

I'm getting a bit bored with this by now, and the two kids are staring with their mouths open, so I start walking towards him. So he says, 'This is ridiculous, I must ask you...' I take my time, and rock slightly on the balls of my feet, the way me old man taught me, and give him one of me stares. I can see the muscle in his jaw clench. He knows as well as I do that he's got no chance, but he holds my stare for about three seconds, and then turns and picks his kid up out of the sandbox, and they head off towards the gate.

I glare after them just in case they turn round, but they scuttle off out the gate with the kid kicking and screaming. When I look back at Joe I've still got the sour look on my face, and he's watching me not sure whether to copy the other kid and start bawling. He thinks he's going to get it in the neck for throwing the sand, but I grin at him, flex me biceps and holler like Tarzan, so he starts to giggle. We have a good laugh. 'Never let poncy types like them push you around.' I say. When I took him home, he says, on the step, before he goes inside, 'See you next week, dad.'

Tommie's Toys

TWO MEN are creeping around the corner of a factory, sticking close to the wall, trying to keep in the shadow of a neon sign which says 'Tommie's Toys'.

Ted: Keep in the shadows you fool. Do you want the whole town to see us?

Bob: It isn't me they'll see. What possessed you to put on a high visibility vest anyway?

Ted: Oh Jesus. *(Takes off jacket and stuffs it into a dark sports bag he is carrying)* I told the missus I was taking the dog for a walk and she nagged me into putting the jacket on, said I'd be knocked down in the dark otherwise. I had to put it on to shut her up.

Bob: So where's the dog?

Ted: I forgot to bring him.

Bob: Great. Won't the missus notice?

Ted: Nah, she'll be too busy watching 'Desperate Housewives'

Bob: Well then, you're the one that works here. How do we get in?

Ted: Round the back to the loading bay. No one will see us there. We can get in through the back door and the safe is just past the photocopier room down the corridor.

Bob: Right you are. I see the loading bay, oh, there's the door. Did you bring the jemmy for the door?

Ted: You said you'd bring that. Where would I get a jemmy? I don't even know what a jemmy is for Chrissake.

Bob: Holy God, what possessed me to bring a fool like you on important business. What's in the bag then, your bloody sandwiches?

Ted: *(Rummages around in the bag and pulls out a large rubber mallet)* I couldn't find a hammer. This'll have to do.

Bob: Ok then, give it a good wallop.

(After some banging they notice that the padlock on the door isn't locked and they enter a dark corridor)

Ted: (whispering) I brought a torch. *(Searches around in his bag again, and brings out a Mickey Mouse torch, puts it on and a faint light shines down the corridor as the torch starts playing a Disney tune)*

Bob: Turn that stupid thing off, I can see better without it. There's a light coming from one of the offices.

Ted: Oh, not to worry, that'll be the photocopy room, they're always forgetting to turn the light off.

(The two men start to creep down the hall in single file)

Bob: I can hear heavy breathing. Is it you?

Ted: Don't be daft, it must be the motor on the fridge in the staff room.

(Suddenly the door of the office with the light is flung open, and a man emerges waving a gun. His shirt is open showing a white vest and his braces are hanging down)

Ted: Blimey it's the boss. Why's his hair sticking up in the air?

Tommie: *(Peers into the darkness)* Who's there? Show yourself or I'll shoot.

Ted: *(drops his bag and puts his hands over his head)* It's me, Ted.

Tommie: Ted? Ted who? And what in the blue blazes are you doing in my factory in the middle of the night?

Ted: *(near to tears)* It's me, Ted who makes the clown costumes. I, um, thought I'd do a bit of overtime.

Tommie: Ted? Oh, bloody hell

(*A woman's voice is heard from the photocopy room)* 'Who is it Tommie?'

Bob: (*smirking*) Looks like you're not the only one doing a bit of overtime.

Tommie: Get out! Get out the pair of you before I shoot. And you're fired. You're both fired.

Bob: You can't fire me Tommie. I don't even work here.

Ted: Christ Bob, let's get out of here. The wife's going to kill me.

(The woman they heard calling Tommie peers out of the door of the office, she's half dressed and clutching her dress in front of her.)

Bob: Well, well, Ted. If it isn't your ever loving.

Woman: Ted? My Ted? What the hell are you doing here? Who's minding the dog?

Ted: I'll talk to you later, my girl. *(Turns to Tommie)* Shoot me will you, eh, not if I shoot you first. *(He lunges for the pistol, points it at Tommie and squeezes the trigger. A small flag falls down from the barrel that reads 'BANG')*

Sonnet

I try my best to make a lovely rhyme,
I study, strain, complain to no avail.
Throughout the years I've given so much time,
And still no canto comes that you could hail.

Iamb, acrostic, free verse or cinquain,
Elegy, haiku, epic lyric, trope,
Canzone or stanza, couplet or quatrain,
Pastoral, ballad, these I nearly cope.

Help me Alexander, John or Seamus
Homer, William, or Emily and Poe.
Neruda, and Yeats, and Spike - all famous.
Muldoon and Durkin, you'll assist I know.

Cause I can't write a sonnet –
Doggone it!

Lightning Source UK Ltd.
Milton Keynes UK
UKOW05f0200051113

220430UK00001B/2/P